MW01595176

Look To Your Light

Look To Your Light

R. E. Robb

authorHOUSE®

AuthorHouse™
1663 Liberty Drive
Bloomington, IN 47403
www.authorhouse.com
Phone: 1-800-839-8640

Published by AuthorHouse   05/16/2013

ISBN: 978-1-4817-5530-6 (sc)
ISBN: 978-1-4817-5527-6 (hc)
ISBN: 978-1-4817-5528-3 (e)

Library of Congress Control Number: 2013909286

Cover Model: Jonah Boswel
IPhotos By: Elsa Moreno Pizarro

Unless otherwise indicated, all Scripture quotations in this book are taken from the HOLY BIBLE, NEW INTERNATIONAL VERSION Copyright 1973, 1978, 1984, 1995, by International Bible Society

Dedication

In John 8:12 it says,
'When Jesus spoke again to the people, He
said, "I am the light of the world. Whoever
follows me will never walk in darkness,
but will have the Light of Life."'

It is my prayer that when in trouble or
doubt, you will look to Jesus.
He is your Light.
Look to Your Light!

Books by R.E. Robb

Love, Money, And Other Persuasive Words
"I Learned About Boating From This..."
The Golden Scimitar
The Light in Dorky Walker

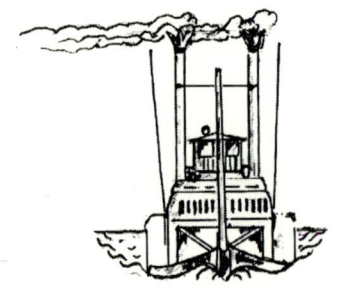

Prologue

In the novel, *The Light in Dorky Walker*, Dorky never knew his father, and was given the name "Dorky" rather than the intended "Darcy" through a nearly-illegible birth certificate application penned by his mother. Later, he survived the deaths of his mother and uncle, and was orphaned.

At 14 years of age, he was nearly drowned in a flooding Mississippi river, and later survived a wreck of the working riverboat, *Killdeer*. The boat was willed to Dorky when he was only 18 years old, after the death of her captain, Jonathan Hannah. Then, Dorky was charged with the murder of a crippled moonshiner. All this after suffering through the death of his Scottish protector and friend, Pastor Jamison MacAndrew (Pastor Mac) of the Kirkcaldy Christian Church in Quickville, Mississippi.

Dorky Walker struggled through his younger years never having someone to call 'dad', and others made fun of his name, but unknown to most, he had his "Light." It shone in the darkness of his closed eyes, and by blinking off and on, it answered Dorky's questions. As Pastor Mac explained, it was the Holy Spirit within him, leading and directing his path since Dorky gave his life to Christ and became a Christian when he was 14 years old. God spoke to Dorky saying that he could call *Him* 'Dad'.

His Light wasn't with him at all times, no more than our parents are always with us. As he matured, there were periods of time when the Light was not at his call. But Dorky kept his faith.

Dorky's friends were few, but loyal. Willie Gilley (*For the first time that I could ever remember, I had a friend with a funny name too,* said Dorky) was his best friend, and Dorky called him "Wil" and he was called "Dor" by his new friend. Wil's father was dead, and his mother married Pastor Mac. Wil went on to school and seminary and took over Kirkcaldy Christian Church when Pastor Mac died.

Jason Jones was the stoker on the *Killdeer*. A large, strong man, he lived aboard the boat in the engine room, even when he wasn't working. Pete was the deckhand and drank too much. He taught Dorky how to drive a car, and although he frequently wandered off, he seemed to show up whenever he was needed.

And unknown to Dorky, Mary Sue Donnovan was hoping for the day when she and Dorky would wed.

Now Dorky suddenly faced another crisis, another challenge, another test of his faith as one night, river fog hugged the surface of the brown, rushing water and melted into the trees on both banks of the Mississippi River like a huge vaporous snake. Above the mist, the tops of the twin stacks of the riverboat *Governor Harlan G.* belched black coal smoke and showered sparks along their course, slicing through the ethereal screen.

Dorky Walker, young Captain of the workboat *Killdeer,* squinted through the darkness as the vague image of the *Governor Harlan G.* on her southward trip, emerged from the fog. Her three decks were aglow with colorful lights, music, and crowds of people partying, dancing, and enjoying a leisurely cruise downriver aboard the luxurious paddlewheel steamboat.

But then, the big riverboat suddenly went dark and silent except for the screams of panicked passengers. The huge craft yawed violently as flames and smoke burst from the lower deck, sending crowds of revellers running blindly in all directions, many leaping into the muddy river.

Chapter One

**When you pass through the waters, I will
be with you; and when you pass through
the rivers, they will not sweep over you.
When you walk through the fire, you will
not be burned; the flames will not
set you ablaze.**

ISAIAH 43: 2

I recognised the *Governor Harlan G.* as she steamed through the fog that night. Her captain, Daniel Wasson, was a gnarly, old veteran of the U.S. Navy, who, it was said, had been dishonorably discharged for smuggling food and goods from Navy ships and selling and trading it to starving Pacific Islanders during WWII. He had been regularly in and out of jail since. I saw him burst out of the wheelhouse and rush down to the main deck just before the sternwheeler ignited.

I yelled down the speaking tube to the engine room, "Jason! Get up here quick! Now!"

The big, black stoker came lumbering up the wheelhouse ladder as Pete, the deckhand, burst through the wheelhouse door. "Did you see old *Harlan* blow up?" he yelled.

"Yeah, sure did! Both of you get out on deck and toss some of those cotton bales to the folks in the water!" I spun the wheel hard to port, heading *Killdeer* for the stricken pleasure craft. "Then get the small boat ready to launch. Hurry!"

"Aye, Captain," they chorused.

The *Harlan* was dead in the water and drifting away from the far shoreline, the passenger's only escape. I headed *Killdeer* for her port side and rammed our blunt prow into the side of the burning ship, shattering our forward loading ramp. I gave her all the power the little workboat possessed, and muttered a prayer as the 185-foot-long sternwheeler began to move sideways toward the shore.

The flames were shooting out of *Harlan's* shattered cabin windows like blow torches. I could feel the heat rising in my wheelhouse as *Killdeer* valiantly pushed. Finally, the other side of the steamboat nudged the opposite shore, providing escape for the passengers and crew.

But it would be too much, too late for *Killdeer,* The bulwarks were aflame, the smell of burning paint and wood filled the wheelhouse with a choking stench, and smoke made my eyes burn and water, and the wheelhouse windows were turning black with the heat. They'd soon shatter, sending spears of glass piercing anything that might be in their way, like me. Sparks, flaming chunks of wood, and gosamer wisps of once luxurious curtains, now in flames, floated ghost-like from the cabins and ballroom. I saw *Killdeer's* big forward cargo mast fully in flames, toppling toward me. I dove through the flaming wheelhouse door and felt myself falling from the upper deck.

"Well, you blundering sack of putrefying swamp slime, you've certainly done it this time, you have!" It was a red-faced Captain Hannah, slamming his cane down atop a tombstone, sending chips of stone and sparks flying in all directions.

My voice was weak and shaky, and I tried to tell him that I didn't have any choice -- I had to try to save those folks on the burning river cruiser, but he wouldn't listen. "You wrecked my boat once before, and I knew you'd finish her off someday. And as sure as a 'gator's got teeth, you did it for certain this time!"

He was drifting off, going farther away, it was getting harder to hear him, and I yelled, "No, Captain, I only did what I......!" but he was gone, and I was yelling into the still blackness of my dream.

I wished that I could have had my Light. It would have given me answers, and I'd know if I done right or not. I squinted hard into the blackness and suddenly, there it was! I started to ask it if I done right by pushing the burning steamboat up onto the shore, but I stopped as it got bigger, growing larger than I'd ever seen it before, and it began to change shape, coming closer and closer until I could see that it was a man, all in white, shining like candlelight.

"Aye, me fine young lad, 'tis good it is to be a-talkin' with ye again!" It was Pastor Mac, all in white, glowing like an angel, his beard trimmed better than I'd ever seen it before, and his eyes as bright as stars.

"Pastor Mac," I cried. "I really lost the *Killdeer* this time!"

"Sure and you did, lad, but the lives you saved are well worth the loss of an ancient old workboat, me boy!" He smiled bigger than I'd ever seen.

"But now I haven't got a boat, no crew, no job. What'll I do Pastor Mac?"

"Well, lad, what you'll do is remember that God is always with you, and you are with Him." He began to slowly fade away. "And He'll never leave you, nor foresake you, me boy. Never! Ever!"

"Don't go!" I yelled. "Please!"

He faded away. I continued to look for my Light, but it did not appear. The darkness was as if I was in the bottom of a well, totally black and still.

I remembered other dreams; my mama, her brother, Unkie, and the town of Quickville where Pastor Mac and I knew so many people, but everything faded away, and I wondered if I'd ever see any of that for real, ever again. Once, I saw light that was different than in my dreams. It was yellowish and seemed to be kind of bumping in and out -- like when sometimes at night I remember feeling my heart beating. Once or twice I thought I heard a noise from outside my dreaming too, like far-off and faint. But I didn't know where I was, or when I'd see things for real again. It was scary.

Far away I could hear a beeping noise. It got louder and louder, and the yellowish light got bright-er, and I could feel my hand move up to my face, and I hurt all over. I was blinking, and slowly began to see real things again; the squares on the ceiling, a wall with a blackboard and writing on it, and the end of the bed I was in, with my feet sticking up like a couple of swamp toads with a blanket tossed over them. I could move my head, and turned toward the beeping noise and saw a funny-looking machine all lit-up with numbers and a jagged line going across the front of it. I realized that I was in a hospital bed.

There was a raspy, growling noise next to my bed. It sounded like a big, angry dog ready to bite me, but it was only Willie Gilley, snoring. His head was hanging over the back of the chair, his mouth wide open like an abandoned rabbit's hole in the woods.

"Wil..." I said with a scratchy voice.

He jerked awake like I punched him in the bel-ly. "Dor!" he yelled, "you're awake!"

I tried to smile and say 'Hi,' but saw a grayness coming around me. My head sagged back into the pillow, and it all went away. I was asleep again.

Sometime later, the light was bright and white, not yellow like before. I lay there thinking that I must be seeing daylight, and the yellow had been nighttime lights in the room. I was almost afraid to open my eyes, in case it all went away again like it did before. Was it days, hours, or just minutes ago that I'd seen Wil sleeping next to my bed? I was sore all over, it was hot, and I was uncomfortable. I tried to move to a better position.

"He's waking up!" I heard someone say. There were other voices, far off, and I didn't recognize any of them. A hand touched my shoulder.

"Dor. Dor. You awake, man?" It was Wil. I opened my eyes and saw that it was daytime, and Wil was looking at me all worried-like.

"Hey, Wil," I muttered.

The others in the room were cheering and clapping and all talking at once, until a big lady in white hushed them with a warning that if they didn't be quiet, they'd all have to go out to the hall.

"Ah, man, how ya feelin', buddy?" said Wil.

"I feel pretty bad." My voice sounded like a crusty chain being dragged across a pile of rocks. "How long have I been here?"

"Don't talk," said Wil. "Just rest and I'll fill you in on all that's happened since you pushed the *Harlan G.* ashore."

I looked around the room and saw Mrs. Gilley -- now Mrs. MacAndews, -- Katie, Wil's wife, Sheriff Sardino, Katie's father, not in uniform, so I guessed that he was not there to arrest me, and Mason Quick, Editor of the *Quickville Courier* newspaper.

Standing quietly in the back was Jason Jones, my stoker from the *Killdeer,* his arm all cemented-up in a cast.

"Jason," I squawked, "what happened to your arm?"

Jason came to the end of the bed, that big smile plastered across his face. "You done fell right onto me, Captain!"

"Jason was in your small boat, the scow, when you fell -- or was blown -- out of the wheelhouse." said Wil. "He tried to catch you to keep you from crashin' into the bottom of the scow. He saved you from more serious injuries, but broke his arm in do-ing it."

"Thanks, Jason," I said, and he shyly looked down at the floor, embarrassed.

Wil went on, "You and your crew are big he-roes, Dor. Your actions saved a whole lot of lives, and newspapers and television all over the country are talkin' about what you did. Our church has had prayer vigils for you every day for a week."

"I've been in here for a week?"

"Sure have, Dor," said Wil. "Folks been here every day too, lookin' in on you and askin' about you."

Sheriff Sardino and Katie came to the bed. "We have to leave now, Dor," whispered Katie. "We're sure glad that you're doin' okay!"

Mason Quick leveled his camera at me and took a couple of pictures. "Get well soon, Dorky," he said, and left the room.

Wil took a stack of newspapers from under the chair. "When you feel up to it, here's a bunch of newspapers with the story in 'em of what you did."

The nurse was quietly moving everyone out, and then began to take my temperature and blood pressure and asking me a lot of medical questions. She did some writing on a clipboard and said, "My sister and her family were on the *Governor Harlan G.* that night, and they escaped onto shore because of what you did." She wiped her eyes. "My name is Susan, and I asked to be your nurse. If there's anything I can do, anything you need, please don't hesitate to let me know." She turned to leave, "and thank you, Dorky."

I began to leaf through the news accounts of the fire and the burning of *Killdeer. Incredible sacrifice..., Noble action...., Heroic, selfless and brave..., National hero..., A spirit of courage..., Gallantry....* Papers from major cities all over America. I was a little stunned, and a whole lot embarrassed.

It was probably twenty minutes later that there was a soft knock on the door, and it opened slowly. Nurse Susan peeked around the edge of the door and said, "Captain Walker, there's a TV news crew here from Dallas, and they have to return in just an hour or so." She looked back and forth and behind her. She whispered, "Do you feel well enough to talk to them?"

"Are you going to be in here with us?" I asked.

"Of course," she smiled.

A man with his ball cap on backwards and a huge camera on his shoulder came in, studying some kind of a hand-held meter, and fiddling with the camera's controls.

A gray haired man in a suit and a big smile was next, followed by a young woman with a clipboard and pen.

"I'm David Daley of KDTV, and we just want the American public to see its newest hero, Captain Walker!" He smiled the big smile again. "Just relax. We'll ask you some questions, and you just answer as you see fit. But remember, what you did was astonishing, so don't be overly modest or shy, okay?"

The camera began rolling, and David Daley's voice went into a deep baritone as he said, "Ladies and gentlemen, I'm David Daley, here in the Mellon County General Hospital in Mississippi where young Captain Dorky Walker is recovering from the crash and explosion of his river workboat one week ago on the Mississippi River near Duvalle."

The camera slowly swung around the hospital room and stopped, its huge glass eye staring right at me. "Here is Riverboat Captain Dorky Walker who is credited with saving more than 60 lives by sacrificing his own workboat by ramming, and pushing the burning pleasure River Sternwheeler, the *Governor Harlan G.* onto the shore, allowing her passengers to escape the burning craft." He turned to me. "Captain Walker, are you able to tell our audience exactly what transpired on the river that dark and fateful night one week ago when you saw the *Harlan G.* burst into flames on the river?"

"Well, Mr. Daley, like you said, when I saw that, I called my crew to make ready and we shoved her over to the west river bank."

"Exactly, Captain!" gushed Daley. "Without regard for his own boat's safety or that of his crew, this noble seaman did the only thing that would save those souls aboard the *Harlan G.*, and that was to ram his sturdy little workboat into the burning inferno and shove it to safety!"

I sat silently until Daley finished, "You are to be commended, Captain Walker, for your decisive, and expert seamanship. There are many people alive now because of your unselfish dedication!" He finished with a sweep of his free hand as if bowing to an audience at a play, "This is David Daley for KDTV, thank you, and good night."

Nurse Susan quickly ushered them from the room, smiling apologetically at me.

I was really tired, so I laid back and closed my eyes. In a moment I was asleep, and the vision of a smiling Pastor Mac was before me. He held out his hands, palms up, as if he was presenting me with something, and said, "Look to your Light, Dorky. Look to your Light." and then he was gone.

Chapter Two

For if you forgive other people when
they sin against you, your heavenly
Father will also forgive you.
                                Matthew 6:14

Doctors and nurses invaded my sleep, and I opened my eyes to see that it was morning already. They had put a new bag of watery-looking stuff on the hanger by my bed, and squirted something into the little hose that was stuck into my arm. I was surprised that it didn't hurt.

But my neck, and my back, and my ribs, they all hurt. Nurse Susan said that she put pain reliever in the hose. Just a few minutes later most of the pain in my body was gone. I said, "Thanks, Nurse Susan." She just smiled, and a doctor explained that I had a lot of bruises, a cracked rib, but no "severe trauma" and I guess that was good because he said I could go home the next day.

Home. I don't have a home. My home was *Killdeer*, and by now she's just a mess of ashes floating downstream. The doctor finished his examination and he and Nurse Susan went out, leaving the door to the hallway open. I glanced up because something moved, and saw a man peeking around the corner. I said, "C'mon in mister."

He was old and bent-over. Dirty clothes were draped over his skinny body, he had a scruffy beard and needed a haircut badly. "Hello, boy," he said in a gravely voice that spoke of years of too much cigarettes and whiskey.

I said, "Hello. Who are you lookin' for?"

"Well, son, I guess that'd be you if you're Dorky Walker."

"Yes sir," I said. "And who might you be?" I figured he'd be someone who was on the *Harlin G.* or had family that was. But he didn't even look right for that.

"Well, Lordy," he said. "You sure enough look like your mama."

"So, you knew my mama?"

"Yup, son, y'see, I'm Walter Walker...your daddy!" He started talking really fast then. "Don't you get all angry at me now, you're sick, y'know, and I read about what you done, and wanted to come see you and get to know you. You're famous now, y'know son, and the news said you were here, so I came straightaway!"

"My *daddy?*" I felt anger clogging up my chest, and my jaw went all tight, like when things don't go so good on *Killdeer*, and I raised-up in the bed, mostly to get a better look at him.

He backed-up a couple of steps, bumping into a chair, and put his hand up in front of him. "Now, now, don't get all mean and nasty just because I been away for awhile!"

I laid back. I'd seen enough of him. This is the man who ran off when I was just a little baby and left mama to get along on her own. She wasn't much more than a baby her ownself. Now he's come back. But I'm not sure I even want him back now after so long, I don't even know the man!

"But I didn't leave her all alone, boy," he stammered. "My brother, Warren, said he'd take good care of her and the boy -- you."

"I never knew no 'Warren' Mister, there was only my Uncle, and he's dead now too."

"Warren told me you called him 'Unkie,' and he *was* your uncle, but he was my brother, not your mama's brother."

I remember wondering why we all had the same last name of Walker, when Mama was married and would have had a different last name than her brother...He was my daddy's brother, not my mama's!

"Why'd you go off?" I asked.

"Well, boy, y'see, your mama was a good woman, but we didn't get along together so pretty good. She was always yellin' at me for havin' a drink or not comin' home at night, and just about everythin' else." He scratched at his beard and sat down hard on the chair. "I just couldn't take no more of that, so I got out of there, that's all."

I laid back and closed my eyes. "So, what do you want?" I asked.

"Well, I figure that since you're famous now, you'd need someone to help you with the travelin' and interviewin' and kind of watch-out for you, y'know, keep the bums from botherin' you, stuff like that."

I was tired and felt like I was about to go to sleep. "Go to Kirkcaldy Christian Church in Quick-ville, and tell Pastor Wil -- Pastor Gilley -- what you told me. He'll take care of gettin' you fed and set-tled-in someplace."

Sometime later, Nurse Susan woke me up to give me a sleeping pill. I asked her if she'd call Wil and warn him about Walter Walker.

That's all I remember of that day.

"Let's see how you handle walking today, Dorky." It was Nurse Susan at my bedside just as I woke up. "We'll see if you really are a 'Walker.'" She laughed a little laugh, and I smiled at her, just because I liked her, not that it was a funny joke.

I was a little wobbly, but we made it around the halls, and by the time we got back to my room I re-ally felt better.

"I think we're probably going to lose our most favorite and famous patient today," she said.

"I'm ready, ma'am."

That afternoon Wil came to take me home. I didn't really know where he would take me since I hadn't had a home since *Killdeer* burned up.

"Katie wants you to stay with us, Dor," said Wil. "We have room for you. You can stay as long as you need to get back on your feet, buddy." Wil was picking up the plastic bag with my stuff in it -- all that I had left in the whole, wide, world was in one yellow hospital bag labelled, 'Personal Possessions.'

"Where did you put Walter Walker?" I asked Wil.

"Who?'

"Walter Walker, my..." I choked-up trying to say 'father'. "He says that he's my daddy."

"Oh, yeah, Nurse Susan called me saying he'd be coming to the church, but he never showed-up." Wil looked at me, funny-like, "You say he's your daddy?"

"He says he is. And he knows about mama and Unkie, and he told me that Unkie wasn't mama's brother at all. He says Unkie was *his* brother."

We were quiet for awhile, then Wil said, "If he is your father, we have to respect that y'know."

"I suppose so, Wil, but it's hard to do because he ran off, never seeing us again or providing anything for mama. And I sure don't want *anything* from him now." I remembered how poorly he was dressed and how shabby he looked. "I wasn't very nice to him I guess. Maybe he moved on to someplace else."

Katie put me up in what used to be Wil's room, before Pastor Mac went to be with the Lord. Being in that house again made my chest ache like I was being squeezed by a giant swamp snake, but I knew it was just the memories of a happier time in this house that were clogging up my heart. I was weak and tired and could hardly get my shoes off as I fell into the bed. I guess I was asleep before my last shoe hit the floor.

Wil woke me up for dinner. "Hey, you gonna snore your life away?"

"Aggh! Go away, man!" but I was awake and wanted to get up.

"Okay, Dor, we'll eat up your dinner and you can starve, old buddy!" he joked at me as I raised up out of the softness of the bed.

I felt better, and Katie had fixed a fine dinner for us. We talked of many things, catching up on our friendship, until the doorbell rang. Wil went to see who was there. We heard some conversation, then the door closed and Wil came back with someone. It was Walter Walker, shaved, hair nicely cut, a new suit, and holding a gentleman's hat cradled in his arm. He looked like a banker or a successful businessman.

"Howdy, son." he said.

"Hello." I squeaked. "Looks like you got all cleaned-up for a big party."

"Yup, and I've got me a room at the Quickville River House. Mighty fine folks here in this here town, son. They are sure proud of you."

"But how did you afford all this?"

"I just explained that I'm your daddy and they all just took care of me fine." he smiled.

"But I mean, how did you pay for it all?"

He brushed the tip of his new shoes on the back of his pants leg, "Well, you got great credit here boy, they're all willin' to let us have anything we need!"

"Credit?" I almost yelled. "I don't have anything any more! My boat is gone, I owe my crew back pay, and I don't have a job or any way of payin' for all of this. I'm stayin' here through the kindness of friends." I was getting madder as I spoke. "You shoulda asked me first before you went to spendin' money we -- I -- don't have!"

"Now, boy, relax." He sat down and picked-up a piece of fried chicken and began to chew on it like a hog gnawing on a ham hock. "I figger you'll be asked to do some interviews on TV and on the radio and they'll surely pay you a handsome sum for that. We'll have plenty of money soon, I'd wager." He stopped chewing on the chicken leg and wiped his forehead with the napkin.

"You alright?" asked Wil.

"Ah, I been havin' 'woozy' spells now and then."

We left the table, Katie helping Walter along by the arm, and went to the livingroom. As was their habit, Wil had a prayer time, thanking God for all of our blessings and for getting me through the water, river and fire as he promised in Matthew 6:14, and for bringing Walter Walker into our lives. He prayed for Walter's health to be improved and that he be watched-over by the Holy Spirit.

Walter sat with his head in his hands, rocking gently back and forth.

The prayer over, Wil and Katie went to the kitchen to make coffee. Walter looked up from his hands and said, "You believe in that prayin' stuff?"

"Yes. After mama died, I was taken in by Pastor MacAndrew and he taught me about the Bible, about God, and praying, and I've seen it work, and I believe in it for sure."

"How about it fixin' somethin' that's wrong with a person's body, y'know, like the 'woozies' that I get? I plum fell over one time, almost broke my head. Woke up four hours later in a Memphis alley." For the first time, he looked unsure of himself, sort of scared and worried.

"God can fix anything, but you gotta believe in him and that he can fix anything, even the 'woozies.'"

"Well, boy, maybe you'll do some prayin' for me, will ya?"

"Sure, Walter," I promised.

"And it'd sure please me, and look better to folks, if you called me papa, or daddy, or somethin' like that, okay?"

"Sure, Walter," I promised.

We had coffee and Wil talked to Walter about the Bible, God's promises, and how we can be assured of a place in His eternal kingdom when we leave these bodies and go to Heaven to be with Him. Walter asked some good questions, and showed interest that surprised me. He had never been told these things, he said, as he left for the evening.

The next day, Wil called me to the telephone in his home office. "It's your Attorney in Barriston who handled the *Killdeer's* books."

"Hello, Mister Bradley," I said. "I've been meanin' to call you, sir, but I've been in the hospit..."

"I know, I know, Dorky, and that's no problem, but there are some things we must discuss immediately. Are you able to meet with me if I come to Quickville? I don't want to talk about these things over the telephone, you understand?"

Hampton G. Bradley, Attorney at Law, was there three hours later, carrying a large manila case and looking serious. He got right down to business.

"Dorky, it appears that the Riverboat, *Governor Harlan G.* was operating on expired permits for carrying passengers, and that her condition was so bad that new permits were being withheld until substantial repairs and modifications were made in order to comply with safety requirements.

"Further, it appears that because of that, her insurance was invalidated until compliance was accomplished. It also is being investigated that the owners were unaware of the lack of insurance, unable to afford the repairs, and deeply in debt, and intentionally destroyed the vessel in order to relieve themselves of these problems."

"Are the investigators going to talk to me?"

"Only regarding what you saw that night. The

question of your vessel's insurance is being discussed since you intentionally rammed her into the *Harlan G.*, thereby destroying the *Killdeer* by a wilful act of her owner -- you."

"But many of the people, the passengers, were saved by what I did, right?"

"Of course, and that's commendable, but it doesn't change the fact that your actions intentionally, wilfully and knowingly destroyed the vessel, *Killdeer*, of which you were master and owner."

He continued, "Normally, the *Harlan G.'s* insurance would have covered your boat's damage or destruction as well, but she had no insurance."

"When do the insurance investigators want to talk to me?" I asked.

"Actually, they should be here just about any time now. It's best that you give them all the information you can, as accurately as you can remember. I'll be with you. In the meantime, I want to go over your financial standing. I have all of your records here." He opened the manila folder.

I was told that there was not enough to buy another workboat, but there was more in the account than I expected. We had just completed talking about what money was left from *Killdeer's* operations when the insurance investigator showed up.

"Captain Walker, I'm Inspector Delgado, and I have just a few questions." He sat at the kitchen table, quite at ease. I was nervous.

He gave a quick rundown of the events that

night and then said, "And what exactly did you see and do, Captain?"

When I told him about the *Harlan G.'s* Captain leaving the wheelhouse before the fire broke out, he looked at me like he'd been told that his pants were on fire. "Are you absolutely sure of that, and if so, would you testify, under oath, that it is totally true and accurate?"

"Yes sir, Mister Delgado, that's surely true as true can be," I said. "It was Capt'n Daniel Wasson."

"Anybody else aboard your boat see him?"

"It's possible that my deckhand, Pete, saw him, but I don't know for sure about that."

He asked a few more questions, thanked us and left.

"I'll keep in touch with you, Dorky," said Mister Bradley, "and let you know what transpires with the investigation, and the insurance claims. Good night."

Walter showed up for dinner that night, and Katie and Wil greeted him like family, which I guess, he was.

"Dorky, I been givin' this God and Bible stuff a lot of thought these past couple of days, but I need more information, more details, y'know."

"What's causin' that?" I asked.

"Well, son, I'm gettin' pretty old, and I think that I might not have many days left, especially since I been having these 'woozies' and fallin' down and such. If there's a chance that I'm missin' out on somethin' other than just dyin' and bein' gone for-ever, I want to know about it. I figure it's like gettin' hot tips at the race track, you just don't ignore 'em."

"That's really good, Walter, and Pastor Wil has a Bible study twice a week, and you'll want to come to the church on Sunday too. There's a lot to learn, so are you willin' to go to them with me?"

"Sure, son, if you start callin' me daddy, or dad, or papa, or pa, or somethin' other than 'Walter.'"

"Okay, Pop!"

Chapter Three

Immediately the boy's father
exclaimed, "I do believe; help me
overcome my unbelief!"
Mark 9:24

To fully recover from my fall, I was told to walk as much as I could, so I walked to the church for the Tuesday night Bible Study. I sat in the back. Walter was in the front row, sitting quietly, watching Pastor Wil speaking his message.

I closed my eyes during the silent prayer segment and asked the Lord; "Father, You told me that I can call you 'Dad' and now I have my earthly father wanting me to call him 'dad,' 'pa,' or 'pop,' and I don't know what to do." I prayed for guidance, and as I was about to mutter 'Amen,' when my Light suddenly appeared, a small speck in the dark vastness of my sight and mind.

"Dad, is that you?"

The Light blinked off, then back on.

"Thank you, Father, for being here for me. What'll I do about Walter, who says he's my father, and you, who I *know* is my Father?

I was filled with God's answer, not in words, for I couldn't hear anything, but just the same, it was suddenly in me, in my heart, in my soul, as if I were a pot, seeded with a plant that suddenly grew to maturity -- His answer:

"As you have said, he is your earthly father, I am your Heavenly Father, but remember, you both are my sons, worthy of my grace. Embrace your earthly father, my son, as you have embraced Me, your Heavenly Father."

My Light blinked off.

"Dang, boy," Walter said when I was leaving, "this stuff is really hard to understand! You know how old this here Bible is? It's a lot older than me, and look how much is in it!"

I agreed, "Yes, pop, there's a lot to learn, are you up to it?"

"I sure don't know if I'm up to it or not, boy. But that Pastor Wil can really explain stuff good!"

"We'll come to church on Sunday, and you'll learn more. But you should also be readin' your Bible whenever you get time. I'll help you with any of your questions. "

"I got one."

"What is it?"

"Well," he scratched his head and put his hands up like he was holding a basketball in front of his face. "How do you know for sure that all this stuff in the Bible is true?"

"It's called 'faith' pop, like when you learn about Jesus and the Bible, you'll just know through faith that it is all true. Then, someday, when one of your prayers is answered, you'll surely know for sure and you'll give God praise."

I didn't know if that was really the best answer, so I added, "You should ask Pastor Wil that question too. He'll give you the best answer."

I left him and walked to Wil's house where I was staying.

The night was warm and quiet. I took care of both by opening the window so I could hear the crickets' songs and feel the cool breeze coming off the Mississippi River. I lay back, thanking God for watching over us all that day, and praying for Wil, Katie, Mrs. MacAndrew, and of course, Walter Walker, my pop.

I remembered what Pastor Mac told me in my dream, so I looked to my Light. "Holy Spirit," I said softly. "Are you there?" The black expanse beyond my sight was solid, unbroken by the slightest glimmer of a Light. I said again, "Father, are you there?" And a small speck of Light appeared in the center of the blackness and soon grew to be a small star in the vast universe of my mind's sight.

"Please help me Father to have the patience and knowledge to be able to help my earthly father be safe and well, and become a believer, Amen."

My Light blinked off, then on again, and began to fade into the darkness until it was gone.

Morning burst through the open window with all of the sounds of the town waking up, automobiles hurrying past, and bright morning sunlight spreading across the room and into my eyes.

Wil was heading out the back door on his way to the church as I came downstairs to the kitchen, lured by the aroma of freshly-made coffee. I always thought of Unkie and of Pastor Mac when the smell of morning coffee hit me. Both had given me coffee when I was really too young to be drinking it. But it hadn't seemed to hurt me none. At least, not yet.

Mrs. MacAndrew was stirring something on the stove, and stopped when I came in. "You be careful around that Walker fella, even if he is your daddy, boy, there's lots of bad people around who'll lead you into temptation!" She began stirring again, "Those folks may not even want to get you into sinnin', but it happens all the same, boy. You just be careful, hear?"

"Yes'm, I'll be real careful!"

I had some cereal and coffee and headed for Wil's church. I found the side door open and no one in the office or worship center. I called for Wil and Pop, but no one answered. I figured that I'd better walk into town an see if I could find them.

It was a warm morning, and the town was quiet. Quickville folks tend to stay inside when it gets hot, unless they have to go to the store or Post Office or some place like that.

I stopped first at the grocery store and asked if anyone had seen Walter or Pastor Wil. No one had. Then, at the Post Office, Mr. Howard from the feed store said that he saw Walter last night, and he was pretty drunk, he said. I thanked him and headed up the road to Doctor Foster's office, figuring that if he had got himself hurt, he'd likely be there.

"Oh, Dor, I'm glad you're here," said the nurse lady, and she took my arm and led me down a hall, into a room, where I saw Wil standing next to Walter sitting on the end of a green table-looking bed thing, staring at the floor. His shirt and his pants were torn and dirty, his shoes were gone. He had bruises on his face and one eye was swollen up bad. He had bandages on his arms, neck, and one leg.

He looked up at me like a dog that had been bad, and knew it. "Howdy, son," he muttered. "guess all these nice clothes aren't much to look at now, are they?"

"Aw, pop, what happened to you?"

"Well, I'm not sure, son, I had a couple of drinks at Eddie's Place. Then I went to rest a bit, and two -- or three -- fellas beat me up, took my shoes and what money I had, and left me crumpled-up in an alley."

"I found him behind Eddie's," said Wil. "Almost had to carry him here. Good thing he's skinny!"

Doctor Foster came in then, "How'ya feelin' old boy?" He was a big, friendly, red-faced man who had been an Officer in the U.S. Army and still looked it.

"I'm sore, Doc," said Walter. "But I guess you knew that, didn't 'ya."

"Yessir, I figured that, and I figure somethin' else too, Mister," he glanced at a clipboard he held. "You better give up the booze, old scout, or you'll be laid to rest with a bloated, busted liver." He turned to leave, "And it won't take much longer, either."

Doctor Foster took me by the arm and led me out into the hall. "He tells me you're his son, Dorky. Is that true."

"Well, yes, I guess it is."

"Well then," he said softly. "You'd better keep him away from the bottle." He thumped his finger on the clipboard. "His liver is 'bout shot, and his heart is weak, and his lungs rattle like a locomotive runnin' down the tracks on square wheels."

"Pretty serious?" I said, then felt stupid. Of course it's serious, or the doctor wouldn't be telling me all this.

"It's serious, and on top of that, he's a pretty old man -- tells me he's 78-years old -- who hasn't taken care of himself at all." He turned and went down the hall, saying, "Do what you can, Dorky. He's a pretty sick man."

"Thanks, Doc."

He turned back to me, "By the way, there'll be no charges for your father's treatment. What you did out there on that river was terrific, young man!"

Back in the room, Wil was helping Walter into

his shirt and pants. "He's gonna have to go barefoot," said Wil. "Somebody made off with his shoes, his wallet, his watch, his…"

"Dignity," added Walter. He was sad, his head hanging, his thin shoulders bowed forward, as we walked him to Kirkcaldy Christian Church.

They went on, and I stopped at the drug store and bought Walter a new wallet, an inexpensive watch, a pocket comb, and a brand-new hat.

I hurried to the Quickville River House to find Walter laying on top of his bed, fully clothed, except for his shoes, a pair of ragged tennies Wil had found for him, were on the floor. Wil sat alongside him.

"How ya feelin,' pop?"

"Like I been hit by a bus." He looked sad, but more alert than when he was at the doctor's.

"Walter wants to talk to us," said Wil.

I took a moment to give him his new wallet, comb and hat. He smiled, "Thanks, son. You're a good boy."

He put the items inside the hat and sat it on the bedside table. "I need to talk to both you," he muttered. "This beatin' scared me, boys, and I been thinkin' that if it happens again, there ain't goin' be no 'next day' for me. I've realized that I'm gettin' pretty dang old, and you and Wil have shown me that there's more to life than drinkin,' smokin,' chasin' around, and connin' folks out of their hard-earned money." He stopped and looked at each of us, I guess to be sure we were listening. "Like I said,

I'm scared. I'm scared -- for the first time in my life -- that I might die. And if...I mean, *when*...I die, I sure don't want to go to Hell like Pastor Wil has told us about." He raised up on one elbow.

"Boys, I want to be a Christian, like you and Wil. I want to do somethin' with my life...if it ain't too late already. I believe. Help me overcome my disbelief."

"God bless you for that, Walter," said Wil.

I just sat there, sort of stunned. He had said almost the exact words of Mark 9:24 when Jesus drove the evil spirit from a man's son.

Wil and I prayed with Walter. He repeated each sentence in his gravely voice asking The Holy Spirit to come into his life, for God to lead and direct him, and thanking Jesus for His sacrifice on the cross that took away all of our sins, when we gave our lives over to Him.

Walter sat with his eyes closed after Wil had finished the prayer. When he finally looked up at us, there was a quieter, calmer look in his eyes. His face seemed different too, less tense, I guess. "Dorky," he whispered, "I want to say that I'm really sorry I caused you so many problems, and thanks for lookin' after me, son."

"Where'd he go, Wil?"

"I don't know, Dor." He shook his head, looking down at the floor. "He was gone this mornin' and I went lookin' for him. He coulda gone north or south, coulda took a bus either way. Anyway, I couldn't find him."

"Okay, maybe he'll turn up in a day or two. I hope he's stayin' sober!"

I left Wil and hurried to the City Hall where I was supposed to meet with attorney Hampton G. Bradley, the owners of the *Governor Harlan G.,* and an insurance adjuster. I was walking, and some people of the town recognized me, probably from the television, and called out to me, saying some pretty nice things. One man stopped me wanting to shake my hand, saying that he had friends on the riverboat that night it caught fire, and they escaped because of what I did. He poked a $100 bill into my shirt pocket and rushed off.

A piece of paper was taped to the City Council Chamber door saying "Governor Harlan G." so I went in. There were about 15 people there, and they all jumped up and clapped, whistled, and cheered when I came in. Flashbulbs popped. It really scared me. They shook my hand and patted me on the back, smiling and laughing. Cameras were clicking and humming.

"We all wanted you to know, Dorky," said Attorney Bradley, "that we consider what you did an act of heroism and bravery, and we thank you." More cheering and clapping. "Please sit down, and let's get on with this inquiry."

Insurance company attorneys, steamship company officials, the River Authority, and a bunch of private folk talked back and forth while a lady took it all down on a little typewriter machine.

A big man in a shiny gray suit called my name. I stood up, and he said, "Are you Captain Dorky Walker of the river workboat *Killdeer?*"

I sort of figured that everybody knew who I was, but I answered him anyway, "Yes sir, but the *Killdeer* is gone. Ya see, she caught on fire..."

"Yes, Captain."   He looked sort of grumpy-like. "Just answer the questions, please."

He asked, "Did you see anything unusual before the fire broke out on the riverboat *Governor Harlan G.?*"

"Yes, sir."   I didn't say any more because he told me not to.

"Well?" he put one hand on his hip and looked like he was waiting for something to happen.   I didn't say anything else.

"Please, Captain, do tell us what you saw." he turned away from me and looked up at the ceiling.

"I saw her Captain, Daniel Wasson, leave the wheelhouse and run forward and down the stairs to the foredeck.   Then the fire started."

"How did you know it was the *Harlan's* Captain you saw?"

"Well, sir," I explained, "I knew him from seeing him many times before."

"Would you recognize him now if you saw him?"

I said that I surely would.   He walked to a side

door, opened it and said something to someone inside. Four men came into the room, all dressed in captain's coats and hats.

"Mister Walker," said the man in the shiny gray suit, "do you see the captain of the *Governor Harlan G.* among these men?

"Yes."

"Well, would you mind telling us which one of them is he?"

"The third man from the left." I said.

There was a lot of mumbling, chairs scraping, and the four men were led out of the room. The man I identified scowled at me like an angry swamp hog.

"Thank you, Captain," said the gray-suited man, now looking more grumpy than before, "You may be excused."

"Wait, Captain Walker," said Attorney Bradley, "We have some unfinished business with which to attend." He talked funny sometimes. He walked over to where I still stood from being about to leave, and held out a big envelope.

"I was just advised that in light of the fact that your workboat, the *Killdeer*, was destroyed and the cargo lost as a result of your act of heroism in saving the passengers and crew of the *Governor Harlan G.,* the Gulf Coastal and Northern Insurance Company, and the Mississippi River Authority are authorizing replacement of the lost vessel and payment in full of the value of the cargo she held when destroyed."

Everyone stood and cheered and clapped, and

more flashbulbs popped. Attorney Bradley, grinning like he just sneaked a big old jumbo shrimp from a gumbo pot, handed me the envelope and whispered, "Now we can get back to work!"

Chapter Four

**And now what are you waiting
for? Get up, be baptized and
wash your sins away, calling on
his name.**
Acts 22: 16

"**H**elena, Montana?"

"No, Dorky, Helena, *Arkansas*." Attorney Bradley sat back in his big chair, smiling. "It's a good price, Dorky."

He had discovered a river workboat for sale up-river and suggested that we go look at it. "The engine is more modern and it'll carry a greater cargo load, and faster, than the old *Killdeer*."

He convinced me that we should look at it, and I asked Wil to go with us. Just as we were about to leave the church, Walter came in the front door, all dressed up in new clothes, a new hat, and shiny black shoes. "G'morn' boys," he said.

"Hey pop, where you been," I asked. "We looked all over for you!"

"I stayed at the River House last night. Figured I'd spent enough time botherin' y'all."

"You're no bother, pop," I said, and gave him a friendly punch on his arm.

"I've been wonderin' about somethin,' Dor," said Wil.

"Wazzat?"

"I've been meanin' to ask you, did Pastor Mac ever baptized you?"

"No," I said. "He baptize you?"

"Sure," said Wil. "In Michael's pond."

"All the time I was livin' there in Pastor Mac's house, the river was all muddied-up and churnin' from being flooded," I explained. "We talked about it, but even Michael's pond was full of mud."

"We need to baptize you, Dor," said Wil. "And you too, Walter."

I didn't know exactly what baptizing was, or what was involved in being baptized, so I said to Wil, "Sure, Pastor Mac wanted to do that to me, so I guess it'll be okay if you do it."

Walter just nodded, like he wasn't quite sure what he was getting into.

"If y'all got bathing suits, go get them, and we'll go over to Michael's Pond and do it!" said Wil.

We met at the pond. It was a really nice, warm day, and the pond was clear of all the flood's mud. Wil hurried us down the grassy slope and we took off our shoes and socks.

"I don't have no bathin' suit," said Walter. He had a pair of pajama bottoms on.

I didn't have a real bathing suit either, but a pair of jeans with the legs cut off would do just fine, I figured.

"Oh, man!" said Wil. "This is so great; a father and his son gettin' baptized at the same time. Halleluiah! Now y'all just sit on the grass there while I tell you about baptism, okay?"

I looked at Walter and he nodded. I smiled at Wil and said, "Have at it, Pastor!"

"Okay. John the Baptist was directed by God to baptize those who repented of their sins, and that act represented the forgiveness and cleansing from sin that comes from faith in Jesus Christ."

He looked at us to see if we understood. Confirmed, he continued, "The submerging in water signifies that we are buried with Jesus, and just as Christ was raised from the dead, we too will live a new life with the Holy Spirit leading and directing us when we are raised up." He looked to see if we understood, and continued, "Walter, you being the elder, you'll be first, okay?"

"Sure, Wil." He said.

Walter waded into the water next to Wil, who placed his left hand on Walter's head, and said, "You are being publicly crucified with Christ and no longer live, but Christ lives in you. The life you live in the body, you live by faith in the Son of God, who loved you and gave Himself for you." He bent Walter backward, under water for about three seconds, then raised him up.

"You have been baptised in the name of Jesus Christ and have turned from your sin and selfishness to serve the Lord. This means placing your pride, your past, and all of your possessions before the Lord. It is giving the control of your life over to Him, Amen."

Walter wiped his face with his hand and said, "Amen!"

I was next, and Wil began the same ritual. I closed my eyes and looked to my light. It was there, glowing more brightly than I think I'd ever seen it before. I said, "Lord I hope this takes!" The light blinked off, then on again...it would take.

We went back to town shivering from the cold pond water, and Walter headed for the River House. I dressed and I rushed to all the stores where Walter had bought his clothes and to the Quickville River House where he rented a room, and collected bills for what I'd need to pay for the things he'd bought, then hurried back to the church.

Attorney Bradley drove his car, and I felt like some kind of important person, rolling along in the big sedan. Wil was quiet, looking out at the passing countryside like he really missed travelling. Kirkcaldy Christian Church had a large congregation, and because of that, it kept him busy there.

It was a three hour drive to Helena, and we got there just as everyone at the boatyard was going to lunch. So we went to eat too. We were in a small, local restaurant, and ordered our lunch. "Y'know, Wil," I said, "at Pastor Mac's church I used to put money into the pan they passed around every Sunday, but I haven't done that since I been back here."

"That's called 'the collection' or 'tithing.'" said Wil.

"Yeah, that's it; 'tithing.' That's what Pastor Mac called it too."

"Well, Dor," started Wil, just as our food got there and he said grace. He continued, "well, Dor, the tithe is used by the church to help needy folk, sick or disabled elderly people, some mothers with children that can't support themselves, and to keep the church workin'."

I tore into my sandwich because I was really hungry, but I kept looking at Wil so he'd know I was listening.

"What some folks don't understand," said Wil, "is that whatever they tithe -- give to the church -- it will be multiplied back to them by God." He chewed on his sandwich and took a drink of his soda. "In Malachi 3, verses nine to eleven, it says something like; 'Bring the tithe into the storehouse, that there may be food in my house (the church). Test me in this says the LORD and see me throw open the floodgates of heaven and pour out so much blessing that you'll not have room enough for it.'"

"But you should give willingly, happily, or don't give at all. Remember, if you give, you'll receive."

I didn't quite understand all that, but I said to

myself -- and to God -- that I'll surely give to the church from now on.

Attorney Bradley pulled into the boat yard, and the big, new car looked as out of place as a hot dog stand in a city dump. The owner, Mr. Downey, met us there. He was a thin, white-haired man who wore those carpenter's kind of clothes with no sleeves and a bunch of pockets all over the legs. We walked out onto an ancient, rotting pier about ten feet above the water. Its boards were black and loose, and I worried that we might just fall right through into the dark, oily-looking water below. Mr. Downey pointed out the boat.

She was tied alongside the old pier, and four big rubber fenders hung down her side, keeping her cushioned from the ragged, black and oily pilings. She was hard to see very well, being so close to the pier, but there was a wooden ladder leading down to her side.

"Y'all go on aboard and look her over. If 'n you have any questions, I'll be in the yard shack over yonder." Mr. Downey pointed to an old barn-like shop building at the edge of the yard.

I went down first and walked across the deck to the other side. She seemed to be stable, not a rolly-polly boat like some I'd been on. The paint and general condition of the woodwork looked very good, and the decks were clean and solid. I headed for the engineroom and was stunned to see two large Diesel engines. There were no boilers or big, dirty piles of coal, only a steel bucket full of dirty, greasy rags. It was pretty clean and didn't even smell bad like old *Killdeer* did.

Next, I headed for the wheelhouse, excited to see what sort of modern layout was up there. I wasn't disappointed. A complete instrument panel, large throttle and shift controls, two marine radios, a fathometer to measure the water's depth, some other electronic-like things I didn't know what they were, and a huge ship's wheel, brightly varnished, that spun easily left and right. Only the hand grips were worn from calloused hands and years of steering her up and down the river. There was an emergency flare gun and a loudhailer, that's an electric megaphone or 'bull horn' used by firefighters and police, in a cabinet by the helm. The windows were clean and it looked like most all of them opened-up for those hot days and nights on the river. There was even a seat that swivelled out for the captain, no old wooden stool like I was used to.

We spent two hours looking the boat over. Wil made me almost jump right through one of the windows when he stuck his head up into the wheelhouse and suddenly said, "Wadda ya think of it, Dor?"

He was more excited than I'd ever seen.

"She's a beauty, Wil." I went back down to the cargo deck where Attorney Bradley was walking around, nodding his approval.

Before we left, I looked over the side to see the

workboat's name. There was no name on the hull or on the cabin side, and I hadn't seen any on the log book or the radio log, either.

I asked Attorney Bradley, "Why do you suppose there isn't any name on the boat?"

"I heard a story that she had a very bad reputation on the river," he shrugged his shoulders and pointed toward the old shop building. "Mr. Downey should know."

"Let's have a word of prayer before we go talk to him, okay?" said Wil.

Attorney Bradley and I agreed, and we kneeled-down on the aft deck of the riverboat. "Dear Father in heaven," said Wil. "We thank you for leading us to this place and this boat and pray for guidance as we proceed with the possible buying of it. We ask that you lead and direct us, and give us counsel. Thank you LORD. We send this prayer in Jesus' holy name, Amen."

During Wil's prayer, I was looking to my light and asked, "Lord, am I suppose to get this here boat?" The light blinked off and back on...His answer was 'yes.'

Mr. Downey's office was in the front corner, inside of the big building, walled-off from the piles of old boat parts, dirty, upturned hulls, rusty engines and a variety of the things an old boatyard amasses over the years.

Asking if we wanted any coffee or cold drinks, he drug chairs for the three of us over to the front of

his ornately carved teak desk. The office was pan-
elled in brightly polished teak, and polished brass
boat parts were hung artistically on the walls. A
single filing cabinet was the only other furniture.
The floor was polished varnished cedar planks, that
would look proud on any yacht. A small air condi-
tioner hummed softly overhead.

"What do you think of the workboat, gents?"
He asked.

I let Attorney Bradley answer. He spoke better
than I could. "She appears to be very well maintained,
and seems to fit the bill for the work with which we
intend to use such a vessel," he said. "However, the
Captain's Log, and the Engineroom Log doesn't give
any history of the maintenance that has been accomplished, nor the hours she has on her since the last
haul-out, engine overhaul, replacement of gear and
electronics, nothing to tell us how soon all that routine servicing will be needed."

Mr. Downey slid two books over in front of Attorney Bradley. "Yes, sir, you're right about that.
The log books aboard the boat have only been on
board since she was turned-over to this here yard by
the River Authority." He shifted in his chair, took
off his glasses and rubbed his eyes. "All of the maintenance records are here, in these invoice books. All
of the work ever done to here was done in this yard,
and this is a record of everythin'. She had a complete
hull survey a month ago, and that's in there too."

He put his glasses back on. I noticed that they

were crooked. "I feel that it's my duty, gents, to remind you again that the boat you're buyin' had a
very bad past. The previous owners were into all
kinds of illegal hanky-panky. Y'all will just have to
be careful while up in these here waters."

"Thanks, we will...If Captain Walker here de-
cides to buy her, when can he take possession?"
asked Attorney Bradley.

"As soon as your check, or bank draught, or
whatever you pay with, clears my bank," said Mr.
Downey. "I have some work to attend to, so you're
welcome to study this paperwork right here, if you
want to." He left the room.

I touched Attorney Bradley's arm. "Can I talk
to you outside for a minute?"

"Naw," said Wil. "You two go ahead and talk
right here, I'll go outside and look at the boat some
more, okay?"

"We may have a money problem, here," I said
after Wil had left.

"Why on earth would that be?" Attorney Bradley looked stunned.

"Well, you know that Walter is my daddy,
right?"

"Yes, Dorky," he said. "What does that have to
do with all of this?"

"Well, y'see," I started to explain, "the shop owners and folks in Quickville are givin' him all kinds of
buying credit because he's got no money, and he's my
pop, and because of what I did on the river, y'know,

pushin' that boat ashore and losin' old *Killdeer*."

I handed him the wad of sales slips and invoices and bills Walter had run up. He took out a pad and pen, and began to scribble numbers, goin' "um-huh, ummm" and "ah-ha," as he did.

Finally, he sat back and pulled his glasses down on his nose, looking at me like I'd just took the last cookie. "Dorky, this is quite a few dollars, but it certainly is not going to affect the purchase, if you so decide, of the workboat."

"Phew," I replied, "then we can still get the boat, even with these bills?"

"Yes, I'll keep them, and issue checks from your business account, paying the amount to each of the retailers."

He stood up, "Mr. Downey, get her ready to go, we'll be back Friday for a test run, and payment in full!" yelled Attorney Bradley.

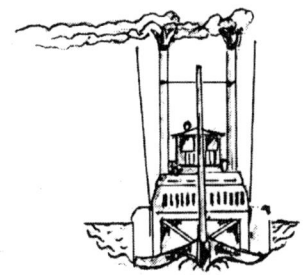

Chapter Five

So the LORD was with Joshua, and his fame spread throughout the land.

Joshua 6: 27

I slept all the way back to Quickville, and it was a good thing that I did, because Katie, Wil's wife, met us when we pulled up to the church with, "Dor! Your father's in jail, and there's a whole bunch of people waitin' for you at the Quickville River House!"

Only half awake, I stumbled up the street to the River House. I went up the old steps, across the creaking porch, and into the brightly-lighted lobby. There were four people there, all in suits and two were carrying brief cases.

"Ah, there you are," said one man, standing and sticking out his hand to shake mine. "Captain Walker, we're here as representatives of The Geoffrey Show on Channel 7, WWTV, to tell you that you are to be Geoffrey's special Guest on his October 25th show."

"That's what, just a couple days off, right?"

"Yes, Dorky," said another man, and handed me a stack of papers, "look these over and make any changes you feel would be appropriate, and bring them with you on the 25th, okay?"

"Sure."

"All of the instructions are in there, and please be on time!" They left, smiling and shaking my hand on the way out.

So much was happening, so fast.

I almost ran to the jailhouse, wondering what kind of mess Walter had gotten into now.

Sheriff Sardino was at his desk and he jumped when I banged in through the door. "Hey, Dorky, take it easy on the building, okay," he said. "Slow down, your pappy isn't going anywhere."

"Sorry, Sheriff," I felt dumb. "Pop okay?"

"Yup, c'mon in back." We went through into where the cells are, and in the first one Walter sat, his head in his hands. His coat laid on the bunk, dirty and torn, and he was in his socks, only one shoe sat by his bed. He had a big, blue bruise under his left eye, and he was really dirty. He looked bad.

"Pop," I said softly.

He looked up, sadness and pain in his eyes. "Well, boy," he muttered. "I did it again. Your old pop sure makes a mess of things, reg'lar like."

"Sheriff, what are the charges that are keeping him in here?"

"Now, Dor," he smiled, "there ain't no charges. He's in here just to get him offen the street." He pulled the cell door open. It wasn't even locked. "Seein' as how my Katie is married to your best friend, Wil, and this here's your pappy, I feel like we's all family. He's free to go."

I got Walter all settled-in at the River House and went to talk to Wil, and to study for the TV show.

Music filled the room and a man hurried from the stage into the curtained side area where I stood. I was waiting to be told when to go out to join Geoffrey, the star of the TV program. The music stopped.

"Ladies and gentlemen," said Geoffrey, "we're proud to have with us tonight a true American hero whose quick action saved many lives on the Mississippi River just fifteen days ago." There was a lot of clapping. "Sacrificing his own workboat, its cargo, and risking his life, this young man pushed a burning pleasure steamboat onto the river bank, thereby allowing 62 passengers to escape to the shore, surely saving their lives. His own boat, as well as the large, luxurious, *Governor Harlan G.* sternwheeler was destroyed by the inferno." He stood up and held his hand out toward me in the wings. "Let's have a big welcome for Captain Dorky Walker!"

Someone pushed me from behind, saying, "Get out there, boy!"

I stumbled out onto the stage, almost falling

down. I got my balance and looked back at the person who had shoved me. The audience laughed and cheered. I felt stupid.

Amid the laughter, Geoffrey said, "I was going to ask you how you got the name 'Dorky,' but I think you just showed me!" The crowd laughed louder.

I sat down in the chair next to his desk and ignored the hand he held out for me to shake.

"First, what do you preferred to be called; 'Captain,' or 'Dorky,' or 'Mr. Walker?'" he said.

"Well, Most of my friends call me 'Dor,'" I said.

"Okay, Dor, we want to be your friends too, because you did a really spectacular, dangerous, and heroic......" He went on to describe the beaching of the burning *Harlan G.* that night on the river, finishing with, "...what were your thoughts when you saw the burning riverboat?"

He had made me a little mad and uneasy with that crack about my name, so I said, very seriously, "Well, of course, I thought that if I saved those people and my boat got burned-up, maybe I would get invited to be a guest on the Geoffrey Show!"

The crowd roared approval and applauded, and Geoffrey sat back in his chair with a surprised look on his face. "And, yes, well, here you are!" He said.

He seemed a little stumped for something to say, and I felt badly about being smart-alecky, so I went on, "I want to thank the Gulf Coastal and Northern Insurance Company for honoring the policy on the *Killdeer*, and making it possible for a replacement workboat to be bought and my business to continue."

Again, the people all clapped and cheered.

Geoffrey smiled at me, "And as most of you know, Gulf Coastal and Northern Insurance Company is a long-standing sponsor of the Geoffrey Show!"

He asked me about *Killdeer*, and how I was able to have her and my river pilot's license.

I told him about Pastor Mac saving me from the river, and my work with Capt. Hannah, leaving out the part about being drugged, and of how the captain had willed me the boat and business. I also mentioned Attorney Bradley and his business.

Geoffrey looked serious and asked, "So what's in the future for you, Dor? I hear that there's a new boat awaiting you."

"Yes, sir, but she's not really new - just new to me, and we're workin' on buyin' 'er now."

"Well, we always like to give our guests a little free advertising on our show," he said warmly, "so, Dor, hopefully you'll tell us the new workboat's name after this pause for a word from our sponsors."

The lights came up and someone was wiping my face and powdering it, and in my mind I heard Pastor Mac's rumbling voice say, 'Look to your Light, Dorky, look to your Light!'

I had been thinking about a name for the new boat for some time. I closed my eyes. My Light was there and I prayed for guidance, and it came to me then as the Light blinked off, and back on.

Back on the air again, Geoffrey said, "Okay, Dor, what name can we expect to see painted on the new boat that was funded by our wonderful sponsor, Gulf Coastal and Northern Insurance?"

"The new boat will be named in joint honor of the two men who saved my life and made it all possible; Pastor Jamison MacAndrew and Captain Johnathan Hannah." The crowd was silent. "And she'll be named the *MacHannah!*"

The silence of the crowd broke into loud cheering and applause, with Geoffrey saying good night over the music, and thanking me for being there.

It was over. I was surprised that through the whole thing, I wasn't hardly nervous at all, until a lady with funny-looking glasses handed me an envelope. I opened it to find a check from the Geoffrey Show!

I rushed back to the River House and found Walter sitting at the desk, reading the Bible. I suddenly felt a new fondness for this old man.

"Hi, son, how'd it go at the TV studio?"

"Pretty good, pop," I flopped onto the bed, and got to the point, "Pop, we've got to get you straightened-out. Man, I just can't keep replacin' your clothes and worryin' about you ending up dead in some stinkin' alley someplace..."

"Hold on there, son," he muttered quietly. "I ain't had a chance to tell anybody what happened to me that got myself all messed-up this last time."

I realized that I never did even ask him what happened. "Sorry, Pop, go ahead."

"I'd left Wil's church and was headin' for the River House, and had to pass that bar where those three whopped me so bad before. They was standin' out front, laughin' and talkin', so I thought they was feelin' good." He rubbed his swollen cheek.

"They jump you again?" I asked.

He got a small smile on his lips and looked up at the ceiling, "No, son, not right away. They didn't hit me and drag me into the alley until after I told them that I forgave them for poundin' on me before, and then I asked them to come to church with me this Sunday."

"Gee, pop, I didn't know that."

"Nobody does son, except them guys and me." He sipped on a soda and continued. "They laughed at me and pushed me around, and then one of them hit me....that's all I remember. And y'know, I don't think they'll be comin' to church real soon like."

I left the River House and headed for Wil's place. It was late at night by then, and I was really tired.

"Dor!" said Wil. "You look terrible, man!" He held the door open for me.

"It's been a long day, Wil, and I just came from Walter's room at the River House."

"How's he doin'?"

"Okay, but I gotta get him outta this town."

Mary Sue Donnavan called right then to tell me

she had watched the Geoffrey Show and happily said that I was 'a very good guest, and did well.'

"We're going to pick-up the new boat on Friday, Mary Sue," I said nervously. "Would you like to go up with us, and then you could ride back downriver with Wil and me on *MacHannah?*"

She sounded very excited as she said yes!

It was Friday morning. Attorney Bradley picked up Wil, Walter, and me and drove us to the boatyard in Arkansas, with a stop in Duvalle to pick up Mary Sue Donnavan. I gave him the check from the TV show. I felt that it was company money.

We met the boatyard owner, Mr. Downey, standing at the pier, looking at the workboat. Two men were aboard, getting her ready for our test run.

"You folks ready to go for a boat ride?" he asked as we walked up. "If everything goes all right, y'all can stay in our cabin tonight, there's plenty of room, and get an early start down river in the morning."

He took me aside, "Dor, remember, this boat has a bad reputation on the river up this way, just be careful, okay?"

One man poked his head out of the wheelhouse, "She's all ready. C'mon aboard!"

The two men cast off the lines and we motored easily from the dock, turned out into the river and for the next hour ran the boat through her paces.

It felt great to be back on the water, at the helm of a boat, even if it wasn't mine. Yet. Attorney Bradley and Walter stood at the bow, talking and laughing, while Wil roamed around the boat and engine room looking for any trouble, and Mary Sue stayed right beside me all the time.

We found nothing wrong with the boat and settled-up with Mr. Downey back in his office. I was back in business!

Attorney Bradley called us over to his car when he was ready to leave, and pulled a large board from the trunk.

"Dor, this is for your new workboat. I saw you on the Geoffrey Show the other night and the next day I had this made up for you."

It was a custom-made, wooden name board to be hung on the wheelhouse. It was beautifully engraved, with fancy designs and the boat's new name was painted bright yellow on it; *MacHannah*.

"That's beautiful!" I said. "Thanks, Mr. Bradley. I'll hang that up before we leave here!"

"Just a minute, Dor," he said, "you seem to be unhappy or worried about something. Anything I can do for you?"

I told him about Walter and the men in Quickville who keep beating on him, and that I wished that I could find a place for him to live and work.

"Well Dor, he's a fine old boy, and I tell you what, I'll drive him on back to Quickville and have him to pack up his things, and he can come to Barriston and work with me."

"Wow, Mr. Bradley, that'd be great!" I was

almost jumping up and down! "Pop, hey, Pop!" I called.

I asked Attorney Bradley, "Where'll he live?"

"I have a big house that just sits mostly empty all the time. It'll be nice to have Walter living and helping out there, and I could use some help at the office too. I'll pay him well." He smiled, "And this check for the TV appearance will just about pay all of his bills from the Quickville merchants!"

Walter came over and they talked for about a minute, then turned and went to Bradley's car, talking and laughing. Walter didn't even say goodbye.

Wil, Mary Sue, and I went back to *MacHannah* and hung the name on the front of her wheelhouse, and began to get ready for the trip. In a drawer beside the helm station, I found a stack of neatly folded U.S. Army Corps of Engineers river charts, out-dated, but good enough for our easy run downriver to Quickville.

I stopped and sat down in the wheelhouse and said a prayer, thanking God for all that he'd done for me that day, I thanked him for Attorney Bradley, Wil, Mary Sue, and even Walter. I opened my eyes to a fresh, new start, ready to begin a whole new life on that old muddy river.

Chapter Six

Those who give to the poor will lack
nothing, but those who close their
eyes to them receive many curses.
Psalm 28:27

Mr. Downey sent his boatyard security guard to
wake us up just before sunrise the next morning.
May Sue was already up, dressed, looking bright and
sunny, and had breakfast ready for the three of us.

I said a long prayer, thanking god for everything, and asking that he watch over us on our jour-
ney downriver. I didn't believe that it was a dangerous trip, but I had some concern about the history
and reputation of the river workboat that had become our *MacHannah*. There may be others who
still have bad feelings about the boat and its old
owner.

The morning air was still, and there was a
smell of mold, foul water, and decaying brush in the
slough that ran up to the old boatyard. We motored
slowly in the dim light of early morning and swung

MacHannah's bow out into the downstream current of the river. The bad smells vanished and were replaced by fresh odors of the slowly flowing river. I had swung the helm seat out for Mary Sue, still leaving enough room for me at the wheel, and said that she could be this trip's Navigator. "You gotta record our speed and course and time and location on the river in that there logbook," I explained. I showed her how to determine all that using the river charts. She was excited, and took to the job immediately and eagerly.

As sunlight swept down into the river's surface, a layer of swamp fog could be seen. It was about a foot thick and seemed to be moving upstream, opposite of the river's current. Occasional debris and tree limbs stuck up through the gray layer, making a path like a boat's wake as the fog moved one way and the water the other. Mary Sue was fascinated, but I couldn't answer her questions about why it did that.

MacHannah was running nicely, making good time, and I was enjoying the smooth, responsiveness of her helm and the ease of piloting her compared to the old *Killdeer*, when suddenly another riverboat pulled alongside at full speed. I looked up just as something smashed into the portside wheelhouse windows, sending shards of glass and pieces of window framework across the room. I shielded Mary Sue, and caught a few nicks and cuts doing so.

I rushed to the portside wheelhouse door just

as someone yelled, "Prager, get you and your filthy pirates out of these waters, or the next thing I throw will blow that tub to kindlin' wood!"

I ducked back inside, "Mary Sue, stay down and try to keep out of sight!" I pulled the helm station cabinet open and took out the emergency flare gun kit, opened it and loaded a 12 gauge flare into it. The flare gun was shaped like a fat pistol, and use to shoot emergency flares high in the sky. The flares burned viciously hot, and would be disastrous for any boat to have one shooting around inside of it.

I saw Wil standing at the rail armed with a wicked-looking boathook, ready to repel boarders.

I took the loudhailer and flare gun and stood in the doorway. "There'll be nary a soul aboard this boat named 'Prager,' and I be named Walker, new owner of the *MacHannah*, heading downriver to our port in Quickville." The loudhailer boomed my words across the quiet waters, echoing among the mangroves along the shore. I lifted the flare pistol and aimed it at the man still standing at his wheel-house door. "Now, if you'd be of a mind to continue this quarrel, I'd be glad to give you a taste of this wee weapon here. And after you're all lit-up and burnin' brightly, I'd be glad to shove you up on yon bank for the day!"

"Walker?" said the man. "You the captain what was on that TV show the other night?"

"Aye, that I am, and this be the *MacHannah*, and there's no 'Prager' aboard her."

"Sorry, Walker, I mistook you for that dirty thief. That used to be his boat!"

I turned to Mary Sue, "Please write-down the name and registration number of that boat." She was smiling a nervous smile.

"Yes, Captain!"

I yelled at the other boat, "Sure and you'll be more than a little sorry when my attorney, Mister Bradley, finishes skinnin' your smelly hide!"

I don't know where my words were coming from, and why I was talking like Pastor Mac, and acting wild like Captain Hannah. I imagined that if I had Captain Hannah's cane, I'd be banging it down too. Mary Sue was looking at me strangely.

The boat turned around real quick like, and pulled away in a hurry.

I got *MacHannah* back underway downriver and called to Wil, "Check the fuel, would ya, Wil?"

Wil took the fuel stick, opened the tank and stuck it to see how much we had left.

"One, four" said Wil. We had just about enough fuel to get to the fuel dock in Lewisport.

The river was still running easily, no storms about to roil her up, and *MacHannah* was riding along, smooth and quiet-like as we approached the Lewisport dock. I was about to swing *MacHannah* alongside the fuel dock, when I saw the dock shack's door close, the shades get drawn, and an "Open" sign get flipped over, becoming a "Closed" sign.

"Ready on the 'midships line, Wil!" I called, and

got an answering wave. I would dock *MacHannah* and see what is going on there.

Wil and I peeked through the corner of the glass door and could see someone sitting at a desk, trying to be invisible, I guessed. I banged on the door. "Hello, in there," I shouted, "I'm needin' some fuel for the workboat *MacHannah*. I be Captain Walker out of Quickville, and I have cash money!"

The blind was slid aside just enough for a weasel-faced young man to peer out at us. Then the door latch clattered open and he stuck his head out. "Wow, you're that guy what pushed that burnin' boat ashore, right?"

"Yup, but right now we need fuel. You goin' sell us some or not?"

"Yeah, sure. I'm sorry Cap'n Walker, I thought this here boat was that bum Prager's." He stepped out of the dock shack and headed for the pumps. Wil uncapped the tank and looked back at me.

"Just 80-gallons, Wil," I said.

The boy stopped at 80-gallons. "If'n we'd had a better welcome, I'd filled her up, 385-Gallons," I told him. He looked like a kicked puppy.

Back in the wheelhouse, I logged the fuel purchase and readied the boat for the next, and final leg of our trip.

I saw something move alongside the fuel dock. A young boy, maybe 12 or 13-years-old was digging through the fuel dock's trash cans. His clothes looked ragged and his hair was long and scraggly like he had been living like that for a long time. I called Wil. "Please take this to that boy, Wil, he looks like he could use it." I handed Wil a five dollar bill.

Wil said a few words to the boy, handed him the money, and headed back to *MacHannah*. The boy stood dead still, clutching the money to his chest and staring at Wil, then the boat, then at me in the wheelhouse as we moved off onto the smooth-flowing river. He was still watching us as I looked back and gave him a salute.

The rest of the trip was routine. No arguments all the way to Quickville, but that boy was on my mind all the way. I remembered that once I was just like him before Captain Hannah taught me the riverboat business. I have been so lucky, 'blessed' as Pastor Mac would have said. I felt a strong urge to help that lad. I prayed for him. And I prayed for guidance to be able to help him.

We pulled into the Quickville slough *MacHannah* fit right into the dock space where we'd kept *Killdeer* tied-up, and there were folks there to meet us. Mary Sue's parents spotted us going past Duville and told the Quickville folks we would be there soon. They had a welcoming committee there for us.

Mary Sue said, "Dor, I was so very proud of you the way you handled the trouble with the other boat and the fuel dock situation," She gave me a kiss on the cheek. "I expected you to get into a fight or something, I guess."

Mary Sue rode back home with her parents.

She had been a lot of help and said that she enjoyed the ride downriver. I hoped we could be together like that again.

Wil needed to go to Kirkcaldy Christian Church and catch-up on his work, so I went with him to help out. While there, I called Attorney Bradley and told him about the attack and damage to *MacHannah* and the registration number and name of the boat that threw the bottle. He said to take the boat to Duke Farley at the Quickville Boat Yard and get it fixed right away, because he had two shipping contracts almost ready to sign.

Wil was arranging the hymnals and Bibles and I was dusting the pews and sweeping-up. I said, "Wil, remember that boy diggin' through the trash cans at the fuel dock?"

"Yup, I sure do. Sad, isn't it."

"I feel like I gotta do somethin' for kids that got no home, or anything else."

Wil stopped and said, "Y'know, Dor, there's a mess of them out there. I see lost kids just about everywhere I go. You and me got real lucky. We were on that road when we were little."

"Yup, we were lucky. I've been thinkin' about how that boy stood there and watched as we left the dock. I'd guess that he'd love to be going with us."

That night, I stopped by the boat yard and told Duke Farley about the boat's damage. He looked at me through the smoke of his pipe, "You just leave 'er where she is, I'll send my boys over to fix 'er up."

After that, I went aboard *MacHannah*. It was my first night of staying aboard and I went to bed that night thinking about what I could do for kids with nowhere to go. It made sense to give them someplace to go. Someplace to learn, and to work if they wanted to. Someplace where they'd always be free to stay or leave. Someplace where they would be safe. And fed. And....

I prayed for that until I fell asleep. My first night aboard the new boat would be spent tossing and turning and thinking about that boy at the fuel dock. I knew what he was feeling. Once, a long time ago, I was feeling just the same as him.

"Dor, Dor! Get up man!" The words tore into my dream and blew away the scattered pieces, letting the morning light form into dazzling brightness. I awoke, squinting into that morning's sunlight, and tried to answer the frantic call, but only mumbled through lips made thick by long, heavy sleep.

"Yeah, yeah! C'mon in, I'll be right there!" I rolled awkwardly out of the bunk and stumbled to the sink where I washed my face with cold water and brushed the residue of unconsciousness from my teeth and mouth.

Wil stood in the cargo area of *MacHannah* looking all excited. "I told Katie about you wantin' to help boys and girls who are out on the streets, and she got real excited, sayin' that's a wonderful idea. She called her father, Sheriff Sardino, Attorney

Bradley, The Donnovans, and my mom, and we're all going to have dinner at our house, talk it over and see if somehow we can do it!" Wil told me what time to be there.

"I'll see you then," I said.

We all gathered at Wil and Katie's house, and for the first fifteen minutes or so, said our hello's.

Katie seated us at the table, and I was next to Mary Sue Donnovan. Sheriff Sardino sat on my other side. Wil said grace.

The talk of ways to help orphaned and lonely, homeless boy's started immediately. Wil's mom, Mrs. MacAndrew, started, "Y'know, that old house of Pastor Mac's is still standing up there on the hill, empty, but in fair condition. With a little work, we could make a bunkhouse for about four or five boys there."

"I think," said Wil, "it would be a great place for boys. We should get started on that, and if we find that there is a need for a similar place for girls, we can do that later, okay? And we need to get work for all of them - keep them busy, and out of trouble."

Everyone agreed.

"I could use some help down at the station cleaning-up and watching the place when I'm gone, sort of a caretaker," said Sheriff Sardino. "And I'd pay 'em too."

Wil added, "The church needs someone to do the grass and bushes and clean-up after the Sunday and Wednesday services. I could keep a boy busy doin' that!"

"I could give a boy or two a job as deckhand on *MacHannah*," I said.

"How do we buy food and clothing for these kids?" asked Mr. Donnovan.

"We'll need to ask the people of Quickville and the local farm people around here for contributions," said Mary Sue.

"Yes," said Mrs. MacAndrew, "we'll need a couple of bunk beds for the house, and volunteers to cook and tend to the place."

"I think we can do it!" said Katie. Everyone agreed.

"Let's get started!" said Mr. Donnovan, "and we'll meet again next Monday, okay?"

"Wait!" said Mary Sue. "I'd like to make a suggestion. We'll need a name for our home for boys, and because Mrs. MacAndrew is letting us use the house, and it was Pastor Mac's home, I'd like to suggest 'MacAndrew House', for its name, unless someone has a better name in mind."

There was no other ideas for what to call our project, so "MacAndrew House" was born.

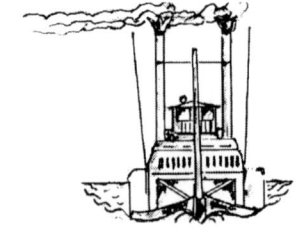

Chapter Seven

For every house is built by someone, but God is the builder of everything.
Hebrews 3:4

N ow that we had the idea, we were going to have to find some beds, arrange for food, buy some clothing, and provide for some boys who most likely have nothing, and what may be hardest of all; find boys who will be willing to live and work in, and for, MacAndrew House.

Sheriff Sardino gave Mason Quick all of the information about MacAndrew House and a list of what was needed. Mr. Quick was grateful for the opportunity to publicise the effort, filling some space in the *Quickville Courier* newspaper. Wil went around to the churches in the area asking for clothes, beds, blankets, whatever the people had to contribute.

Mary Sue and I went up to the old MacAndrew house to see what it needed. First, it needed a lot of cleaning, some repairs, but it would be a great start for our MacAndrew House.

Back at *MacHannah's* dock, two of Duke Farley's woodworkers were repairing the broken wheelhouse windows, and inside I could hear the boat's telephone ringing.

"Hello, this is Captain Walker."

"Hello, Dorky, this is Hampton," a familiar voice said.

"Ah, Hampton....?"

"Yes, Hampton Bradley." he laughed. You forget me already?

"Oh, Attorney Bradley! I'm sorry I didn't know it was you, and no, I haven't forgotten you, sir." I felt silly. "How's Walter doin'?"

"He's fine, Dork, helping out a lot. We have a consignment to carry six tons of railroad engine parts from Lancerton up to Lewisport. They need it by the middle of next week. We handle that okay?"

"I can be in Lancerton tomorrow evening if it'll be ready to load." I was hoping to be able to find some help, at least a couple of deckhands, by tomorrow.

Attorney Bradley said he'd let me know that night if the parts would be ready to load the next evening.

I walked down to the small harbor area where Farley's Quickville Boat Yard was, taking the back streets and checking all of the likely campsites where I might find a boy, maybe two, who I could hire for this job, and maybe make them the very first of our MacAndrew House kids.

In a treed area behind the boat yard, I heard a strange sort of squealing sound and ducked through the bushes to see what it was. There, squatting by a small fire, was a boy of about 16-years old, blowing on a harmonica, and watching a can heating on the fire.

"Pretty music!" I said softly.

The boy jumped to his feet and said in a shaky voice, "I ain't doin' nothin'!" He stepped back like he was about to run off.

"Whoa, man!" I said softly. "I'm not here to chase you off or anything. Just relax, My name's Dorky. Dorky Walker."

He relaxed a little and said, "I'm just fixin' me some of this here soup, then I'll be goin' on."

"Look, I don't want you to leave, in fact, I'm looking for someone to help me on my riverboat. I'll pay you and feed you some good chow, and there's even a place where you can live for free - a real house - if you decide to work with me on the boat."

"I don't know nothin' 'bout boats, mister, but I'd sure like to have a job and some monies and some-place to stay." He sat back down and slipped the harmonica into his shirt pocket.

"Well, I can use you if you want to work," I explained. "And actually, I need two deckhands, so if you know of another boy about your size, I can put both of you to work.

"I got one friend I run with once in awhile, but he ain't been around for a couple days."

"That's okay," I said. "We need to get started early in the mornin', so if you want to do it, c'mon down to the *MacHannah*, and you can sleep aboard tonight."

We walked to the boat yard and I pointed out *MacHannah* to him. He was impressed with the boat, and said that he might like to try working on her.

About an hour later he knocked on the side of the boat. He told me his name was Jonah.

"Okay, Jonah," I said, "there's no whales that I know of in the ole' Mississippi, so you'll be safe!"

He just looked at me like I was talking in Chinese or something. "You know about Jonah and the whale in the Bible, right?"

"No, sir, I don't know nothin' 'bout that."

"Ah, well, we'll talk about it in the mornin', sleep good," and I bunked him down in the galley like I'd been berthed on *Killdeer*. I heard his harmonica.

I awoke early and got the engines started, lit the running lights and prepared the radio and checked all the controls in the wheelhouse. I showed Jonah how to cast-off the dock lines and coil them, ready for use when they were needed.

I checked the clock, entered the time in the log book, and yelled, "Jonah, cast-off the docklines!"

"Someone's runnin' and yellin', sir cap'n," he said.

I went to the wheelhouse door and saw Pete,

waving his hat and running up the dock. He jumped aboard. Grinning, I called to Jonah, "Okay, Jonah, now you can cast-off!" The moaning harmonica sound stopped.

Pete came up to the wheelhouse, puffing. "Thanks, Dor, I sure didn't want to miss goin' with you!" *MacHannah* slid smoothly out into the river's current, swung her blunt bow downstream, and picked-up speed.

"Pete, you're amazin' man!" I gave him a quick punch on the shoulder. "How do you always know when we're headin' off on a job?"

"Well, you're *always* headin' off on a job!"

Lancerton was down-river from Quickville, and with the current pushing us, we made good time. I found room to tie-up at the city dock, and was able to fuel-up there. I went to the dockmaster's office, signed in, and paid the docking fee.

"You did good, Jonah," I told the boy. "Here's some cash so you can get some lunch. Be back here in about an hour, okay?"

Pete said, "Hey, wait up, man, I'll go with you!"

I had to stay with the boat to watch the loading and help-out where I could. It went smoothly. The dock workers were experienced and fast. With some time to spare, I walked on into town, bought a chocolate bar and a soft drink for my lunch, and sat on the steps of a building that looked to be a courthouse or city hall or something. I could see all the way up the main street. I saw some activity in front of an old building, and it looked like some workmen were dragging beds out of the place. I hurried there.

It looked to be an old fire station, and it was about to be torn-down. The windows were being taken out, and doors, and maybe ten or twelve bunk-beds were being stacked out in front. A man was leaning against a truck, smoking a cigarette.

"Scuse me," I said, "what are you going to do with all those old beds?"

"They're goin' to the dump. You want 'em?"

"How much for 'em?"

"You want 'em, you take 'em," he smiled.

"Okay!' I gave him one of the *MacHannah* business cards Attorney Bradley made for me. "Leave 'em right there, and we'll start moving them to the boat right away." I was excited and was talking 'way too fast.

"What you goin' to do with 'em?"

"There's a home for boys in Quickville that needs some beds, and these are perfect!"

The man said, "I'm Jack Grace, and I was in a boy's home once, a long time ago!" he turned and yelled at a group of men stacking doors. "Hey, you guys! get over here!"

He must have been the boss, because four men ran over. "Take these here beds and 'matteraces' to where this man has his boat. He'll tell you where to put 'em. Now git with it!"

They stood looking at me, waiting for instructions. "We're goin' take 'em to the city dock." I took one end of a stack of three beds. "Let's go!"

I was busy lashing-down the stacks of beds and mattresses on *MacHannah's* foredeck when Pete and Jonah came back from lunch.

"What ya got piled up there, Dor?" Asked Pete.

I explained about the MacAndrew's House, then, "Let's get ready to get underway. We've got a long run up to Lewisport." They headed off to prepare for the two-day trip upriver. I went to the dockmaster's office and called Wil. "We'll be dropping-off some beds for MacAndrew House tonight," I told him.

I checked the cargo to see if it was lashed-down securely, took another look at the beds on the foredeck, and went to the wheelhouse to get ready to get underway. I made a log entry, then stepped back and closed my eyes, praying, "Lord, you are awesome! Bringing us here and providing the beds for the House, and from a man named Grace! Your Grace blesses us at every turn, and I thank you, Lord, for providing for us, leading us, protecting us. I send this prayer in Jesus' Holy name. Amen."

My Light was there. It winked off, then back on. God heard my prayer.

The river was running strong, and it took almost all of *MacHannah's* power to get her out into the current and headed upstream. I checked the charts and steered her to the deepest part of the river, where the current would be the least strong. She picked-up speed, and I was able to back-off on the power some, saving wear and tear on her engines, and saving fuel as well.

Pete and Jonah came up to the wheelhouse and I let Jonah take the wheel. He put his harmonica away and was excited to have a chance to pilot a river workboat. He did well, with me giving him a word of advice here and there. I remembered how I felt when Captain Hannah would tell me that I done good. It really made me happy.

"Good job, Jonah," I said. "I don't think it would be very hard to make a real riverboatman out of you!"

He smiled the biggest smile I've ever seen him smile, "Thanks, Mister Captain!"

I felt a stab of anger hearing that, just like Captain Hannah must have felt when I said 'Aye, Captain, sir!'

"Just make it 'Mister' or 'Captain,' Jonah, not 'Mister Captain,' okay?"

"Yes sir, Captain, ah...sir," he stuttered.

MacHannah had a barometer hanging in the wheelhouse, and I watched it carefully while underway. I noticed that the barometric pressure had dropped since we left Lancerton, and the sky was darkening. "Pete," I called, "pull some tarps out of the locker on the port side and let's cover those mattresses on the foredeck, please."

"Aye, Mister Captain Sir!" He ran laughing

down out of the wheelhouse before I could throw something at him. I could hear him still laughing as the locker door banged below.

Moments before Pete came back up to the wheelhouse, rain began to spatter on the windows and making dimples on the water surface. The sky got darker, and the rattle of the rain on *MacHannah's* cabin became louder and more steady. The wheelhouse windshield wipers, even at full speed, were barely able to keep the windows cleared enough to navigate the river.

"Got 'em covered just in time!" Said Pete.

"Where's Jonah?" I asked.

"I donno, I'll go find him."

Pete returned to the wheelhouse a couple of minutes later. "Dor, I think we got a real nut-case on our hands with this Jonah character!"

"Why's that?"

"Well if you look out the port door, you'll see," he smiled.

I gave him the helm, and cracked the portside wheelhouse door open enough to see down along the deck. There was Jonah, naked as a snake, standing in the rain, rubbing himself with a wash cloth.

I yelled, "Jonah! What are you doin'?"

"Well, Mister Captain, I ain't had a bath for about two weeks, so I thought this'd do me for awhile." He had no idea that there was a shower in the boat's head (bathroom) with hot water, soap, and towels too.

I said to Pete, "That boy sure reminds me of me when I was his age!"

The rain slowed and finally stopped just as we slid up to the Quickville dock.

"Line's secure!" Yelled Jonah.

Wil and three others from the church were there to unload the beds and mattresses. Wil came up to the wheelhouse. "Dor, this 'MacAndrew House' is takin' off like a scalded buzzard! We have the town's folks contributing all kinds of stuff. Morgan Construction is addin' a big bunkhouse and bathroom and showers onto the old house, Carl and Edward are puttin' up a fence to make a corral behind the place, a mess of ladies gave us a ton of kitchen stuff, and you got these beds! Man! This is excitin'!"

"And I got a poor boy to be one of our first... um...what are we goin' to call them?"

"Well, we'll be teaching them about the Bible and Jesus, so I guess we could call them 'Students' until we think of something better," said Wil.

"How about 'bairns'? (pronounced *bayrns*). Pastor Mac told me that a Scottish minister in Duddingston Kirk called his congregation, "ma bairns" meaning 'His children.'"

"I like it!" Said Wil. So 'bairns' it became.

Chapter Eight

**The prudent see danger and
take refuge,
but the simple keep going
and pay the penalty.
Proverb 27:12**

It was dark as we eased *MacHannah* out into the river's current. We'd have to run all night and might not be into Lewisport until noon the next day. Depending on how quick she was unloaded, we might be running *MacHannah* back to Quickville the next night, empty. But the water was like a sheet of bronzed glass, glistening, flat and smooth. Occasional splashes of feeding fish broke the surface, and broke the boredom of the long, slow trip. 'Gators launched themselves from the river's bank with a great splash at our approach, either frightened or hungry - but I couldn't imagine a gator being scared of an old workboat, and it sure wouldn't be a decent meal for them. Maybe we just woke them up.

Pete climbed up out of the cargo deck, "Where's Jonah?"

"I haven't seen him since we left Quickville," I said. "I hope he didn't leave."

"I'll go find him," said Pete angrily.

I looked out onto the foredeck, and as far as I could see down the side decks, but there was no sign of Jonah. I listened for the sound of his harmonica, but there was none.

A few minutes later, Pete came back and showed me a piece of the handle of one of the long boat hooks we use on deck. "Look at the marks on this, Dor."

There was a row of deep gouges and the end look to have been bitten-off. "Dear Lord!" I said. "Jonah must have been poking it at an alligator. It looks like it's been chewed off." I pulled the throttle back and spun the wheel. "We gotta go back and see if a 'gator pulled him overboard, and if we can find him!" I shouted.

"Yeah," said Pete. "If there's anything left of him to find."

I turned on the two big spotlights and aimed them on both river banks. I let *MacHannah* drift back downstream in the current, the engines quietly idling so the we could hear Jonah if he yelled - If he was still alive.

Three hours of dead-slow drifting put us almost back to Quickville and where I'd seen the first of the 'gators splashing into the river. I turned *MacHannah* around, gave her some throttle, and started back upstream, still looking for Jonah. I was giving the horn a short blast every three minutes or so to attract Jonah's attention if he was on the bank, looking for us. Pete was on the foredeck, watching and calling out for him.

We had gone back upstream a full two hours, and had just about given-up on finding Jonah or any sign of him, when I heard the now-familiar off-key and mournful sound of Jonah's harmonica, and a flat-bottomed scow came out of a small cut in the bank and headed for us. As it neared, I could see two men aboard. I slowed as it pulled alongside and one of the men climbed aboard *MacHannah*.

"Pete!" I yelled, "what's goin' on down there?"

If Pete answered me, I didn't hear him. Then the wheelhouse door swung open, and there stood Jonah, all wet, muddy, and shivering. "I done fell offen' the boat, mister captain, sir."

"Yeah, I guess you did." I left the wheel and hugged him, "Thank God you're okay, we thought a 'gator got ya."

"Naw, the 'gator got the end of the boathook, but he was so busy achewin' on it, he didn't see me fall in and swim ashore! I saved my 'monica though!"

Pete came up to the wheelhouse then, shaking his head and mumbling about what a dumb kid we had here.

"Take Jonah down to the head and show him how to work the shower, and get him a towel too, okay?"

"Aye, mister captain sir!" Laughing, Pete ran out of the wheelhouse, again too fast for me to throw anything at him.

I got *MacHannah* back up to speed and continued on our way to Lewisport. The river ahead was clear, and now a bit of moonlight was shining on the water. I closed my eyes. There, in the black heaven of my eyesight, was one bright star, my Light. I thanked God for the decision to go back and find Jonah, and asked him to guide and direct us, keep us safe and well, and accept my prayers and praise of him.

My Light blinked off, and back on. I knew that the rest of our trip would be safe.

As the morning sunlight began to filter through the cypress, magnolia, and boxelder trees along the east bank, *MacHannah* stubbornly cruised on, steady and sure. I was beginning to really get attached to this river workboat. She was different than *Killdeer*, smoother, quieter, and more responsive to the helm.

I guided her up the still river and watched the day brighten, and suddenly felt lonesome. I wished I had Captain Hannah alongside me, even if he was mean, angry and loud. And I really missed Pastor Mac too. *MacHannah* didn't need a stoker like *Killdeer* did, and so Jason's big, quiet smile and his friendship was gone too. I still had Wil as a friend, but he was busy at his church and couldn't be chugging up and down this old river with me. Besides, he had a wife and a home now, things I didn't have.

My thoughts turned to Mary Sue Donnovan. I felt a peaceful warmth as I remembered her. I didn't know about love, but I sure felt something for her, and it was a lot different that how I felt for anyone else.

As the day warmed-up, the river got busy with all types of working boats and pleasure boats, and I was kept busy dodging sailboats that seemed to not see *MacHannah*. The traffic made the time go by fast, and soon we were coming up to the Lewisport municipal pier as the sun dropped out of sight, and the city's lights came on, and *MacHannah* nudged the pier. "Line's secure!" Yelled Jonah.

I called Attorney Bradley and he said he'd send the crew over to unload *MacHannah*. He also said for us to stop at Barriston, 60-miles downriver, and pick-up a load of chicken feed bound for Mr. Howard's feed store in Quickville.

An hour later, a crew came and unloaded the crates of railroad engine parts. I was glad to see them go, their weight really bogged old *MacHannah* down.

I checked to see that the boat was tied-up well and closed-up, as Jonah, Pete, and I went into town for some dinner. We hadn't eaten much on this trip, and we were all hungry. The talk at dinner was about MacAndrew's House, and all that we were going to try to do for the youngsters that had no place else to go, and no one to look out for them. Both Jonah and Pete thought it was a great idea. Our bellies full, we headed back to the municipal pier.

"Whoa!" said Pete. "Where's the boat?"

I couldn't believe what I *wasn't* seeing! The

pier was empty, no boat, nothing was there! *MacH-annah* was gone! I ran to the Dockmaster's office, but it was closed for the day.   The River Authority office was open, and I rushed in, surprising the clerk at the lone desk in the small office.

"C-c-can I help you?" he stuttered.

My workboat, the *MacHannah*, was tied up at the municipal pier right over there," I pointed to the empty space, "and now she's gone! did you see who took her?"

"No, I didn't see her leave, but you say she was stolen?"

"Yep, right out from under our noses!"

"I'll call the County Sheriff's Department Water Patrol," the clerk said. "It's their jurisdiction."

"What's that mean?" asked Jonah.

"It means that they are the ones who handle this sort of thing, not the local police," I explained.

When the clerk finished calling, he said, "Wait out there where the boat was tied-up, they'll be right over."

The patrol boat sped up to the dock just as we got there, and I explained to the patrolman what happened. He wrote down a lot of information, and said that they would contact us if anything turned-up.

I told him that the boat belonged to a man named 'Prager' until just a few weeks ago.

"Prager!" He almost yelled it. "Alright, I got a good idea where to look. You'll be hearing from us....

Prager! Agggh!"   He left in a hurry.

All we could do is contact Attorney Bradley and explain what happened, and try to get back to Quickville to wait for news of *MacHannah.*

"Wait at the River Authority," said Attorney Bradley, "and I'll be there in a couple of hours. I'll put a call into Sheriff Sardino in Quickville. I know it's out of his jurisdiction, but perhaps he can help."

I thanked Attorney Bradley and sat in the River Authority's office to wait it out.

Pete slouched in a chair, sound asleep, and Jonah was restless, fidgeting and asking me questions.

"You was goin' tell me about the whales in the river." he said.

"No, what I said was there's no whales in the Mississippi River, so you don't have to worry about bein' gobbled-up by one like Jonah in the Bible was."

"He was 'gobbled-up' by a whale? In a river?"

I gave him a short version of the Jonah Bible story, and finished up with, "So, you see, you'd better do what God says, or you'll be in big trouble."

"But how do I know what He says?" he asked.

"I'm goin' to get you your very own Bible, and you can read about God, Jesus, the Disciples, and learn about how to be a good Christian boy."

"I don't read so good," he said sadly.

"There's a lot of folks who'll help you, Jonah."

He seemed satisfied with that, and sat back

looking at a magazine. Some time later he said, "I want to be a Christian boy, and stay with you at the Andrews Place."

"That's great Jonah," I said. "You'll be our first bairn, and I'll do my best to learn you to read better, but remember, it's the 'MacAndrew House', okay?"

Then my curiosity made me ask, "How'd you happen to be all alone, without no family and all?"

"I guess I never had no daddy, and momma got married-up with a man who didn't much like me," he explained. "I didn't like him much either. He use to hit momma, and one day he kicked me, so I just went away. No place in particular...just away from him. Momma didn't seem to care that I left, so I didn't feel bad about leavin' her alone with him."

"Well, there'll be nobody kickin' you as long as I'm around," I told him.

He wiped at his eyes, and said, "Thanks, Dor."

I heard a car door slam, and Attorney Bradley came in. "Any news on the boat, boys?"

"No, sir," three of us said together.

"Okay, well, let's get on back to Quickville, but first I have to stop at the feed store and see if I can arrange to have that chicken feed delivered to Mr. Howard's store."

There were six big bags of feed, and Attorney Bradley had four loaded into the trunk of his car, and two in the back seat. Pete and I sat in the front seat with Attorney Bradley, and Jonah squeezed in on top of the bags in the back seat. We headed down the road for Quickville. "You okay back there, Jonah?" asked Pete.

"Sure, it's very comfortable!"

After unloading the feed at Mr. Howard's, I went to see Sheriff Sardino. "No news on *MacHannah*, Dor," he said, "but I've alerted all the River Patrol stations all the way to Southern Arkansas, we'll find her."

"I think Daniel Wasson, captain of the *Governor Harlan G.* mighta taken her. He was really angry at the hearing," I suggested.

"Nope, Wasson's in jail."

"Oh, well, how about this 'Prager' guy?"

"I checked on him too, but he's locked-up tighter than a roll of dimes. You're just goin' to have to be patient, Dor, we'll find your boat."

That's when I discovered that I am not patient. Not at all. I went to Wil's house and asked Katie if she could make me up a picnic basket with food and drink that'd last me for maybe three or four days, and that I'd pay for it, then I went to see Duke Farley at the Quickville Boat Yard.

"Mr.Farley, you still have that little outboard motor boat?"

"Sure," said Farley, "you be need'n it?"

"I'd like to rent it from you for a few days, if you can get along without it."

"You just take it whenever you need it. I got little use of it this time of year, besides, there's other skiffs around I can use if need be." He unhooked the ignition keys from a board behind his desk. "And there'll be no talk of 'rent' Dor, you just use it!"

I motored over to the fuel dock and filled the two fuel tanks, then tied it up at *MacHannah's* dock. Katie had the basket ready, and Wil asked me where I was going in the dark. "I'm goin' take a little river cruise, and poke around every inlet, slough, and cut in the river 'til I find *MacHannah.*"

"You goin' tonight?"

"Sure am, but I've got to dig-up a good flashlight before I go."

Wil went out to the shed and returned with a light. It was too big to be called a 'flashlight,' it was a lantern, I'd say. I bundled up with a heavy jacket, a hat, and a pair of wool gloves, and headed upstream, slowly, surely, to find my boat. It was 7:30 p.m.

At midnight, I was past Duvalle and had motored into and out of at least twenty coves. I was warm and fairly comfortable, but I was getting sleepy. I splashed cold river water in my face, and sipped on the thermos of hot coffee. Two a.m., and I passed Barriston with no sign of *MacHannah*, or any other boat that looked the least bit like her.

An hour above Barriston, I came upon a boathouse large enough to hide *MacHannah*, in a dark and quiet slough. I eased up to the two large wooden doors, and shined my light through the crack, lighting up the inside of the boathouse. It was empty.

Another couple of hours, just before sunrise, I was chased away from another boathouse by a pair of big dogs. I circled out into the river, and returned by stopping the motor and paddling up to the doors. It had a boat inside, but its varnished wood reflected that it was not *MacHannah*. I escaped just as the dogs came back barking and snarling again!

It was a long run from Barriston to Lewisport, and I had emptied the first tank of fuel. I'd need to stop soon and refuel. I saw the gas dock where we stopped on the first trip and where I'd seen the boy digging in the trash barrels. The same weasely-faced boy filled up both tanks, and I continued on upriver along a mostly barren area with only occasional farms and no side channels of the river.

It was noon as I began to see inlets and sloughs on both sides of the river. I was nearing Lewisport. The river had narrowed, and the current was faster and strong enough to almost stop the little boat. I found a depression in the river bank covered by overhanging branches and tied off to them. Hidden, I laid back and slept. I wanted to do my searching in the dark, when I would be less likely to be seen.

I didn't sleep very well because of the rocking of the little boat by the wakes of bigger boats passing, and the sounding of their horns. I woke up just before dark, splashed water on my face, ate a little, and drank some cold coffee.

For the next two hours, I worked my way upstream, searching both sides of the Mississippi. There was no place where a workboat the size of *MacHannah* could be hidden. I needed to get out of the cramped boat and stretch my legs and walk some. I was still aching something terrible from my *Killdeer* injuries.

I pulled into a side water where I saw an old shed up on the bank with a pair of railroad tracks coming up out of the water and leading up to its door. There was a light on inside. I felt I had to see what was inside that old boat shed.

I shut down the outboard motor and paddled up to the overhanging walkway and tied the boat out of sight. I waded to the bank and climbed out. It felt good to exercise my legs, even in the cold water. The lantern in hand, I watched to see if anyone or any dogs were around, then made my way toward the shed. The ground was soggy from the rain, and mud oozed into my shoes. It felt cold and mushy. I slowly moved up to the door, but could not see in. On the north side, I found a window, but it was so dirty I couldn't see through it either. I went to the back where there was another door, but again, I couldn't see in. Finally, on the south side, a chunk of the window was broken out, and I could see inside.

MacHannah sat there on a boat trolley, and I could hear men talking and working.

"Don't move, Jack, or I'll bust your skull open with this club!" I stood real still. It was a man's voice, all gravely and mean-sounding. He grabbed the lantern from me and tossed it into the bushes.

"Okay, Snoop, move real easy-like around to the front door." I did.

"Get in there!" he gave me a shove, and I stumbled into the shed, almost running into *MacHannah's* bow. I looked up to see Mr. Downey from the boatyard in Helena. He didn't look happy. He looked worried and confused as he nervously twisted a small book he held in his hands. "Oh, Captain Walker, you've put us in a tight spot, showin' up here like this," he muttered.

No one was holding me and I thought if I jumped Mr. Downey and twisted his arm behind him, he might...I gave up that idea as I looked at the man standing behind him, and the one standing behind me. They were big and mean-looking. I remembered what it said in the Bible, I think it was Isaiah 49; *He made my mouth like a sharpened sword, in the shadow of his hand he hid me; he made me into a polished arrow and concealed me in his quiver.* I took that to mean that I might be able to talk my way out of this...maybe.

"Well, I'm glad we found *MacHannah*, that's the important thing, and when the rest of my crew and Attorney Bradley, and County Sheriff's Department Water Patrol shows up here in a bit, y'all should be gone out of here," I tried to look serious, but I was shaking bad inside. "I'll tell them that there wasn't anybody around when I found *McHannah*."

Mr. Downey said, "Lock him up in the generator room, Michael."

The man behind me grabbed the neck of my shirt and shoved me across the shed and into a dark, smelly room, smaller than the forward cabin on *MacHannah,* and slammed the door behind me. I heard a latch rattle closed. I stood by the door waiting for my eyes to start seeing in the darkness.

I sat down on the floor and waited. After awhile I could see a little bit of the room. Slivers of light were seeping through gaps in the door frame and around a pipe that went out through the roof. I guessed that it must be the exhaust pipe for the generator.

I could hear work being done on *MacHannah*, and wondered what they were doing. I slept for awhile, and woke up in the morning when I heard the door at the back of the shed shut and a lock click closed. I figured that they must all have left.

I stayed quiet for awhile and looked into the black tunnel of my closed eyes, praying that my Light would be there for me. It gradually appeared, like the headlight of an approaching train at the far end of a tunnel. "Father, I'm in a bad spot here, and I pray that you'll help me find a way out of it." My Light blinked off, then back on again. Then, the words came into my mind, into my head, I didn't hear anything, it was like I had a thought, put there by someone else. "Look up to your Light, Dorky, look up to your Light!"

Chapter Nine

**Rise up, LORD, confront
them, bring them down; with
your sword rescue me from
the wicked.**
                              Psalm 17:13

I opened my eyes and looked up to the ceiling, seeing a halo of light around the exhaust pipe sticking up through the roof. "Thank you, Father!" I said.

I felt around the floor and the generator, looking for some sort of tool I could use to get out of there. Under the generator, I found a rusty, bent screwdriver. It was pretty big, big enough to use as a pry bar or weapon. This would be The Lord's sword and I'd use it to be rescued from the wicked, like the Psalmist said.

That exhaust hole in the roof looked to be the only place large enough for me to get out. I stood on top of the generator, and it felt like there was a metal covering for the hole around the pipe, probably to cover a large hole to prevent the hot exhaust pipe from catching the wooden roof on fire. I tried to force the screwdriver under it. Finally, I found a place where it went in between the metal and the roof, and I pried on it, bending it down and letting more light into the room. I kept working the screwdriver around the metal, gradually prying it open. I grabbed the exhaust stack, happy that the generator wasn't running, making the pipe hot, and pulled up on it. It slid apart, and I carefully climbed down and laid it on the floor. I was being as quiet as I could, in case someone was still in the boat house.

A bit more prying on the metal, and it came loose, leaving a pretty good-size hole. I didn't know if I could fit through it or not, but I sure was going to try.

I raised my arms up over my head and stuck them through the hole. I was able to get my arms on the roof and strained to raise myself up through the hole. I fit up to my belt, and was stopped there. My pants would have to come off. I lowered myself back to the floor, took my pants and shoes off and rolled them and the screwdriver into a bundle. I climbed back on top of the generator and sat the bundle out on the roof, and again pulled myself up and through the hole. The ragged edges of the hole scrapped my sides, and I almost lost my underwear, but finally, I popped up onto the roof, out of the building.

I tossed my pants and shoes down onto the dirt below and slid off the roof, landing in mud. I walked over to the dock and saw my muddy footprints from when I first got there. I figured that they'd seen them too, and followed them down to the boat hidden under the walkway. I was sure that it would be gone.

I found Duke Farley's boat upside down on the bank with the motor and fuel tanks gone. I put on my pants and cleaned my feet as best as I could and put my socks and muddy shoes back on. It looked like I'd be walking a long way.

A big, red, ball of sun burned down on me as I walked into a small town probably four or five miles down the road. The sign at the edge of town said 'Woodhill'. There was a diner open, and I found out there was a Sheriff's Department Water Patrol just at the end of the street.

"Stolen boat, huh?" said the officer at the desk.

"Yessir, the *MacHannah*, and I found it in a big boathouse a few miles up the road."

"Hummm, let's take a look," he opened a green book. "Yup, *MacHannah* was reported stolen. Who are you?"

"I'm Dorky Walker, her owner and captain, and you can check on that through Attorney Hampton G. Bradley in Barriston."

He spun around in his chair so fast it startled me. He snatched-up a microphone from a big, black radio set behind him and alerted all available patrols to come to the Woodhill station where I'd lead them to *MacHannah*. "You can find the boathouse again, can't you?"

"Yessir."

He opened another book and dialed the phone. "Mr. Bradley, this is Officer Davidson at Woodhill SDWP, and I got here a young man, Dorky Walker, by name, saying he's the skipper of the stolen vessel, *MacHannah*. Can you verify that information?"

"He says you are who you say you are. Now, the patrol will be here shortly, just tell the boat captain what you told me, and take him to where the boat is, got that?"

"Yessir, and thanks!"

Thirty five minutes later we pulled into the cove and tied up the patrol boat to the dock. The boat captain, Sgt. Charles, said, "You stay here and don't move unless I tell you to."

I was pacing back and forth, nervously waiting for the boat captain, when he came down to the dock, looking at me strangely. "Nope, fella, there's no boat in that boathouse."

I jumped out of the patrol boat and ran up to the boathouse. He yelled, "Stop now, or I'll shoot!"

I ducked inside the boathouse before he had a chance to shoot, and was shocked. -- He was right, *MacHannah* was gone. Again.

"I should handcuff you and shackle your feet, and make you lie face-down on the deck!" He was angry. "Don't you ever do a dumb thing like that ever again -- you could have been killed! What were you thinkin'?"

"I was thinkin' that *MacHanna had* to be there. She *was* just a few hours ago."

"Well, she ain't now," he grumbled, "and you'd known that if you'd have paid attention to the boat dolly they floated her off of, sittin' right there in the water!"

Back at the Woodhill Station, officer Davidson also gave me a stern talking-to. I was glad that Attorney Bradley had shown up to take me out of there.

He drove me back to the old boat house, and we searched around and found the outboard motor and fuel tanks, and Katie's empty picnic basket in an unlocked shed. Attorney Bradley helped me put the motor on the boat and get it into the water.

"Now, Dor, you just motor back on down to Quickville. I have a private investigator that I'll get onto *MacHannah's* trail and I'll let you know when we find out anything."

"Thanks," I said. "I'll call you when I get back to town." I shoved-off and started the engine for the long run downriver.

I laid-back on a couple of seat cushions, and let the river carry the boat downstream at a pretty good speed. By just using the engine idling at slow speed, just for steerage, I figured I could make it all the way to Quickville without having to fuel-up. The sun was warming me, and the steady hum of the engine lulled me to sleep, but for only minutes at a time. Anytime I was nearing boat traffic or turns and curves in the river, I'd sit-up and stay awake.

I had lots of time to think, and my thoughts

were heavy on the side of MacAndrew house and the boys who would be given a better chance at having a successful life by being there.

I came to the fuel dock run by the weasel-faced kid, and slowed, looking for the lone boy I'd seen there before. I knew it was unlikely that I'd see him again, and I was right. I pulled back out into the river and continued on to Quickville.

I truly love that old river. I like the work of skippering a workboat, the independence, and the people, well, most of them. But lately I've had a different feeling. I guess I've been thinking of Captain Hannah, and how he lived his whole life putting water under the bottom of a riverboat. He never really seemed to be all that happy. It was almost as if he wished he was someplace else, doing other things. I guess a lifetime of shuttling cargo up and down a waterway can get to be pretty boring. I also thought that an old working riverboat is not a proper place to expect a wife to live, and to raise kids. It's a solitary, sometimes lonely life, and I wondered if I was outgrowing it just like I did the nightmares of my youth.

All these thoughts brought me to a single solution; I would pray for guidance and help from God.

The sky had darkened, and the crickets began their nightly melodies as I slid the boat up to the boatyard's dock in Quickville. I was stiff and cold, and looking forward to the walk to Wil and Katie's house.

"Hey, Dor!" said Wil. "We've been worrying about you. Did you get *MacHannah* back?"

I told him of all the events of the past couple of days, ending with, "Nope, she's been taken someplace, and Attorney Bradley has a detective lookin' for her." Just then Katie brought me a plate of chicken and dumplings.

While I dug into the meal, Wil told me about the progress at MacAndrew House. "It's amazing, Dor," he said. "People have been bringing things every day, and Morgan Construction has finished the bunkhouse and bathroom they built onto the back of the old house, and Carl and Edward finished-up the corral fence, and went ahead and built a small stable, it'll hold maybe three or four horses or cows I guess. The Quickville ladies have completely redone the kitchen and put in all sorts of pot and pans and a toaster oven and towels and soap and stuff!" He stopped to take a breath, and stole a piece of chicken from my plate.

Katie came with a glass of iced tea for me. "Katie," I said. "Don't you ever feed this man of yours?"

"I could spend my whole day stuffin' food into that man's gullet, and he'd still want more." She playfully mussed his hair as she went back to the kitchen. Wil snatched another piece of chicken from my plate.

"Okay if I stay with you folks tonight?" I asked.

Wil stood-up. "Dor, you never have to ask that, this is your house as long as you want. We love having you here, and besides, where you goin' if you don't stay here?"

"Thanks, man, you're a great friend."

"Brother," he said.

I pulled my plate away before he could grab another hunk of my chicken.

I almost didn't recognize MacAndrew house! It had been repainted, new doors and screens on the porch, and the inside had been turned into a very comfortable boy's home. The kitchen shone like a diamond, and there was a dining room area, and a wall had been put up making a den. Beyond that, the new room had the six double bunk beds set-up, and a bathroom with showers. Katie told me that the mattresses had been cleaned, and bedding had been donated by the local women's club. Along one wall stood a row of lockers, one for each bed. MacAndrew House could handle 12 kids already!

I was thinking about what I could do, when I heard the door close behind me. Jonah stood with his hands stuffed into his pockets, looking at me like an angry billy goat. "Hey, there, buddy," I said, "how you doin'?"

"Why'd you go without me, Dor. I was left all alone here!"

"C'mon, Jonah, Pastor Gilley and Mrs. Gilley was here for you, and you had the whole McAndrews

House for your own self!" I sat down on a bed. "You had food and a place to sleep, Right?"

"Yeah," he said. "But I wanted to go with you to find the boat! I'm your 'deck man,' ain't I?"

"No, Jonah, you are my 'deck hand' and when we get *MacHannah* back, you'll have your old job back. But I didn't want to with me because I didn't know if it would be safe for you, or not." I stood up and got us a soft drink from the refrigerator to share. "And it was dangerous, pal. I got tossed into a little room by the gang that stole the boat, and had to break-out and go to find a sheriff. I never did get *MacHannah* back!"

"The gang hurt you?"

"No. But I couldn't risk having you gettin' in that fix." He seemed satisfied with my answer and lightened-up a bit, sat down and sipped on his drink.

Jonah had his bed all made-up and his clothes hanging in a locker with his name on the front, and had been given the job of taking care of things when Wil and Katie were not there. He showed me around and was real proud of the place.

Katie showed-up bringing Jonah's dinner, and the three of us talked about MacAndrew House, and all of the plans for it. Jonah talked with his mouth full of food, but neither Katie nor I corrected him, because in fact, his enthusiasm was good to see.

Katie and I walked back to the house. "You know, Dor," she said. "Mary Sue Donnovan really likes you. How do you feel about her?"

"Well, Katie," I stammered a bit. "I think she's a great little gal, and I like her a lot. The times we've been together have always been really nice, y'know."

"Yes. Well," she said, "Why don't you take her places, you know, to a movie or dance or out to dinner, or do something to spend some time together. You never know, she might be the best thing to ever happen to you in your whole life."

That night, I heard Jonah's harmonica squeeling as I flopped back onto my bed and read the Bible. I looked to my Light, "Lord, is Katie right about Mary Sue?"

My Light blinked off and back on. It's true.

Then, thinking back over the past days of looking for MacHannah, my eyes were drawn to Jeremiah 39: 17-18. It says:

'I will save you; you will not fall by the sword but will escape with your life, because you trust in me, declares the LORD.'

"Amen!" I said out loud.

Chapter Ten

**'The glory of this present house will be
greater than the glory of the
former house,' says the
Lord Almighty. 'And in this place
I will grant peace,' declares the
Lord Almighty.**
Haggai 2:8-10

I t was a bright morning, and Sheriff Sardino and
Katie came to MacAndrew House with two boys.
They were real quiet, and needed a bath, and their
clothes were really dirty.

"These here fellas are goin' to be takin' care of
the Sheriff's Station, keeping the place clean, and
helpin' me out in the office," he said. "This here's
Chris, and the tall one there is Davey." I said 'Hi' to
them just before Katie took them to find some clothes
that would fit, give them soap and towels, and lead
them to the showers.

"They been in trouble?" I asked.

"Nope, found 'em sleeping in old Grady's barn,
and they said they're lookin' for work, so I took them
in."

We walked out onto the porch. "I ain't one to
gossip," said Sheriff Sardino, "but Katie is sure try-

in' to get you and Mary Sue attached to each other."

"I know, Sheriff, and I really like Mary Sue, but I don't know quite what to do."

"Well, that's simple...call her and start hangin' out with her, and give her a present once in a while, and take her to dinner, stuff like that!"

I sort of stuttered again, "Yeah, okay, I guess I can do that."

"Y'know," he said, "Katie and Mary Sue have become pretty good friends, and I'm told that Mary Sue wants to work with Katie at MacAndrew House." He smiled at me, "what'ya think of that?"

"Well, it'd sure make it more handy than drivin' all the way to Duvalle to take her to dinner, I guess."

Katie came out on to the porch. "The boys have cleaned-up pretty good, and have picked-out the beds they want and are putting their things away in the lockers." She held up a laundry bag, "I'm going to go wash their clothes for them. I'll be back in a couple of hours. Can you stay with them, Dor?"

"Sure. Ah...will Mary Sue Donnovan be coming here?"

The sheriff and Katie looked at each other and smiled. "Yes, Dor. Tomorrow." They left.

I turned to go into the house when I heard a yell and a crashing noise. I rushed in and saw Jonah on the floor with Davey on top of him. Jonah yelled, "I'm gonna kill you!"

I lifted Davey off Jonah and picked Jonah off

the floor.

"I don't know what's goin' on here," I growled, "but whatever it is, I don't like it !"

I had both Jonah and Davey by their collars, and they were struggling to get loose. "This jerk took my pillow!" yelled Davey.

Jonah said, "Did not, I just wanted to use it for a minute, and besides, he took my harmonica!"

They quit struggling, and I let them loose. Davey picked-up his pillow from the floor and took a swing at Jonah with it.

"Stop it Davey!" I shouted. "And Jonah, we don't 'borrow' anything that belongs to someone else unless we ask them if it's okay. Give Jonah back his harmonica, Davey. Okay?"

He nodded, looking down at the floor. "He's a jerk!" he mumbled.

"Okay, you guys, we're going to have a little talk about how to get along with each other and the first rule, Davey, is we don't call nobody names, got that?" He nodded.

About then, Chris came out of the bathroom. I said to him, "Chris, these guys have been fightin' and I'm goin' to have a little talk with them about how to act here at MacAndrew House. You can stay or not - up to you." He flopped down on a bed and said he'd stay.

For about the next fifteen minutes, I told them how they should get along with each other, and sort of made-up a bunch of rules, like, no fighting, no cussing, no taking other's stuff, and no name-calling. I also said that if those rules, or any rules, were broken, they'd have to do extra work, like cleaning the animal's messes out of the corral and shed. They all moaned at that.

"There'll be rewards too," I told them, "if y'all are good, we'll all get to do things like go to a movie, or get ice cream, or go swimmin' in Michael's pond, but you have to treat each other right. No fightin' or you might find yourself back out in the cold."

They were all very quiet, and so I said, "I want y'all to pray with me, Okay?" No one spoke, they just looked at me, so I started, "Our dear Heavenly Father, thank you for bringing us four together and providing this house, the food, the beds and for protecting and leading us and teaching us your ways. We ask that you continue to bless us all, in Jesus' Holy name, Amen."

Chris said, "You believe that stuff?"

"What *stuff?*" I asked.

"Prayin'." he said.

"Chris, if I didn't believe it, I wouldn't do it. And if you try just a little, you'll discover, with help from us here at MacAndrew House, that prayer will get you through the tough times, and bring you good stuff from God."

It was pretty quiet the rest of the day with the boys getting along. Jonah was quieter than usual, and I suppose he was still a bit angry, but we spent some time talking and that seemed to calm him down.

It was just starting to get dark when I heard a noise in the kitchen and went to find Katie and Mary Sue taking groceries out of a couple of bags. "Hi, whatcha got there?"

Mary Sue ran over to me and hugged me. "We've got food for the men of this house!"

"Good," I said. "Maybe it'll keep these guys from fightin'."

"Well, you'll have some help with that," said Katie. "Daddy's on his way over here, and your daddy, and Mr. Bradley too."

I heard the smooth purr of Attorney Bradley's big, fancy car pull up outside of the kitchen, and heard doors slam. I went to the door.

Attorney Bradley came in carrying a large, flat package, and my pop was behind him with another package like the first.

Everyone said Hello, and I gave pop a hug. He looked real good, not so skinny and wrinkled. He said, "Son I made som'thin' for your new boy's house here." He handed me the package.

"That's great, pop, but I gotta tell you, this isn't *my* boy's home, it belongs to all of us."

Attorney Bradley said, "That's right Dor, but without you, it never would have happened." He held up the other package. "Open these up, Dor. "Your father made them, and you're going to be very surprised!"

Mary Sue came over with a knife and scissors

and helped me open the first one. It was a framed, glass-covered, and beautifully printed Bible verse;

> Come, my children, listen to me;
> I will teach you the fear of the Lord.
> Whoever of you loves life
> and desires to see many good days,
> keep your tongue from evil
> and your lips from telling lies.
> Turn from evil and do good;
> seek peace and pursue it.
>
> Psalm 34: 11-14

"That's to hang where your boys will always see it," said Attorney Bradley. "And Dor, Walter here made that special for you all. Turns out, he's quite an accomplished artist!"

Everyone clapped, and thanked Walter for his work.

The other package was being opened by Mary Sue. It was another framed poster Bible verse;

> 'The glory of this present house
> will be greater than the glory of
> the former house,' says the
> Lord Almighty. 'And in this place
> I will grant peace,' declares the
> Lord Almighty.
>
> Haggai 2:8-10

The printing was beautiful, and around it, there were fancy designs, all of them making the words stand-out and made the whole thing look like a work of art. Which, I guess, it was.

While the women were deciding where to hang them, Wil showed-up. He was impressed with Walter's work too. "You be interested in doing some of those for our house and church, Walter?" Wil asked.

Walter shyly said, "Sure, I will, Wil."

I put my arm around his shoulders, "Man, you sure surprised us tonight, pop!"

He look a little embarrassed, "Ah, son, I felt like I ought to do som'thin' to thank y'all for all you've done for me."

"Did you pick-out those Bible verses?"

"Yup, I hope you like 'em," he said, smiling.

"Sure I like them -- in fact, I love 'em!" I said. "How come you're not working as an artist or painter or somethin' along them lines?"

He looked down at the floor, "Well, you might not have noticed, son, but I had a bit of a drinkin' problem, and my hands used to shake real bad, so I couldn't do anything well. That was before -- now I'm a *Steady and Ready Freddy!*"

"Come eat, y'all!" came the call from Katie from the kitchen. I went into the sleeping area and had the three boys wash their hands. I waited for them. They were all talking and laughing together, so I figured the fighting was over. For now, anyway.

As everyone was getting seated, I asked Attorney Bradley, "Any news about *MacHannah?*"

"Not a word, Dor. The investigator should be checking-in tomorrow, maybe he'll have something to report."

Just then Wil came in the back door with two boys 10 or 11 years old. "Sorry I'm late, Katie," he said. "Got room for a couple more fellas?"

The plates and chairs were shuffled around to make room while Wil introduced the new kids. "This here is Harry and his little brother, Larry." Everyone clapped and said 'welcome!' to them. "They'll be your newest bairns!"

I had to explain about Pastor Mac telling me that a Scottish minister in Duddingston Kirk called his congregation, 'ma bairns' meaning 'His children'. "Wil said he liked it, so if it's okay, the boys will be our 'bairns'."

Everyone seemed to approve of that by the general mumbling and nodding that went on.

We finally got seated, Wil said Grace, and we-ate, the bairns digging-in with enthusiasm!

"How many boys...*bairns,* I mean, you got now, Dor?" asked Attorney Bradley.

I told him, "There's five right now, but Wil says he's doin' some talking with an orphanage that's 'way overcrowded, so we may have some more pretty soon."

The food was good, but the bairn's table manners were awful. We'd have to work on that when we had our daily meals. But it wasn't a big deal.

It was late when Wil, Katie, Sheriff Sardino and May Sue left. Attorney Bradley and Walter decided to stay overnight since we had only five of the twelve beds filled, leaving beds for seven more bairns at MacAndrew House. The bairns were asleep as soon as they laid down their heads. We sat up talking until well after midnight.

I laid back on the bed, listening to the breathing and snoring and grunting of the bairns and the men sleeping. I felt a longing, a desire, to be back aboard the riverboat *MacHannah*, with her gentle rocking, the creaks and groans boats naturally make, and the sound of the crickets and pond frogs competing with each other on the banks of the river slough.

I had never considered what I'd do if *MacHannah* was never found. I guess I'd stay here at MacAndrew House, taking care of our bairns, but surely a river workboat the size of *MacHannah* would be impossible to hide. I felt that she'd be back for sure. Some day.

I heard someone or something moving across the room. I figured it was one of the bairns heading for the bathroom. I saw a dark shadow of one of the boys, carrying clothes and shoes going toward the door. He went out, and I got up.

I found him sitting on the front porch, putting on his shoes. I quietly went and sat on the step next to him, and he jumped like I was a redbelly water snake about to bite him. "Whatcha doin' Chris?" I asked.

"Ah, well, I was thinkin' of movin' on." he muttered.

"Don't like it here?"

"It's okay, except for havin' to sleep in there with them other guys."

"Where do you want to sleep?" I asked him.

"I donno...I'm not used to bein' around other people. I usually sleep away from other folks."

"Well," I said, "how about we drag your mattress out onto this here porch, or better yet, out in the shed. There's hay out there. Makes a pretty good bed. You should stay here, because you and Davey have a job working at the Sheriff's office, right?"

"Yeah, and he's gonna pay us too!"

"Well, that's what men do, Chris. We work, and we don't break promises to those who hire us."

"I'd sleep better out in the shed." he said.

We moved his mattress out to the shed. He bedded down and said, "Thanks, Mister Dor, this is better."

Back in my own bed, I closed my eyes and prayed, thanking the Lord for helping me help these kids. My Light was there, and I asked it if I would ever get *MacHannah* back. It blinked off, and then on again...I would get *MacHannah* Back!

Chapter Eleven

**Do not be quickly provoked
in your spirit, for anger resides
in the lap of fools.**
Ephesians 4:25-27

In the morning, both Katie and Mary Sue came
to MacAndrew House and made breakfast for Attorney Bradley, Walter, and me. Then they started
breakfast for the bairns. I went back into the sleeping area, woke up everyone and showed them how to
make their beds.

Out in the shed, Chris' mattress was shoved
into a corner and he was nowhere around. I checked
the corral, then walked out into the woods where I
thought I heard a noise.

I found Chris by a small creek, throwing rocks
at a bird's nest high in a tree. "Whoa! Chris! Man,
don't do that. That's cruel and needless!"

He jumped and dropped the rock he was about
to throw. "You scared me, Dor!"

"Yeah, well, I'm glad I scared you. That's really a lousy thing to be doing, Chris. Those birds are
God's creatures just like you and me, they deserve
to live here in peace, just like you and me. Why on

earth would you want to hurt them?"

"Aw, they're just a target. I wanted to see if I could hit 'em, that's all." He didn't look like he was a bit sorry.

"Well, pal, someday we will all have to answer to God for our actions. Do you want to have to tell him you killed his birds? Man, I sure wouldn't want to have to do that. Now, please go get your mattress, take it to the bunkhouse, your breakfast is about ready."

I was angry with Chris, but had cooled-down by the time I got back at the house. The food was on the table, and the bairns were waiting for me. Chris came in and sat down as I said the prayer; "Dear Father, thank you for this food, this beautiful morning, and for the opportunity to be with your children enjoying your grace. Please watch over us all today, and bless our friends and neighbors who, through you, Father, have provided all of this for us. Amen."

After breakfast, I checked the bairn's room to see that they had all made their beds and were keeping the place clean and sort of neat. Chris' mattress was tossed in a wad on the bed.

"Chris," I called, "You need to make your bed before you go to the Sheriff's Office!"

"Why you pickin' on me all the time?" he complained.

"I'm not, man. Look at everyone else's bedding." He looked. He went and made his bed mumbling that if he didn't sleep in it, he shouldn't have to make it up.

"Pop," I said to him before Attorney Bradley and he left. "You did a really good job on those posters for the house. I didn't know you had such a skill."

"That's what I did for a lot of years, son. You need any more, let me know."

We shook hands, and then I grabbed him and gave him a hug.

"Thanks, son," he said, and wiped at his eyes.

That evening, when Chris came back to MacAndrew House, I had a row of cans set-up on the corral fence, and a bucket-full of good-for-throwing river rock ready for him in the yard.

"Here ya go, pal. You got a bunch of targets and a lot of ammunition," I told him. "Practice your rock-throwing all you want, but don't be tryin' to kill anything, okay?"

He knocked down all of the cans, slept in the shed, and made-up his bed real nice the next morning.

Mary Sue came and fixed breakfast for us, and Attorney Bradley called to say that the private investigator had not found *MacHannah* yet, but had a lead on where she might be. Sheriff Sardino had hung the two framed verses, one at the front door, and one in the dining area. Wil was gone on a retreat with church pastors for a couple of days.

I was helping Mary Sue with the clean-up. She looked worried and asked me, "Dor, is Harry alright?

I mean, he's very quiet, and never talks -- won't even answer my questions."

"Y'know, I haven't ever tried to talk with him. You say he won't talk to you?"

"That's right," she said.

I went back out to the eating area. Harry was looking out the window. "Harry, would you please bring the rest of these dishes into the kitchen for us?"

He said nothing. I went back to the kitchen. A couple of minutes later Harry came in, carrying the dirty dishes.

"Thank you, Harry," said Mary Sue. He didn't reply.

I took him aside. "Hey, buddy," I said, do you know what 'rude' means?"

He nodded, looking at me with sad eyes.

"Well, y'know that not answering ladies when they speak to you is very rude, and we want all of our boys...bairns, to be polite, not rude."

He just looked down at the floor.

"Can you talk, Harry?"

"Uh huh."

"Okay, in that case, I want you to be polite to people. Talk to them, especially ladies, and they'll like you a lot more, and you'll feel better too."

"Okay," he mumbled.

"Good, now go say thanks to Mary Sue for feeding us all. Can you do that?"

"Uh huh." With his hands in his pockets and

looking down at the floor, he went to Mary Sue, and I barely heard him say, "Thank you for the food, miss." She gave him a hug.

Before he left, I said, "Harry, if you want to talk to someone about anything, you come see me, okay?" He actually gave a little smile, and nodded.

Mary Sue finished-up in the kitchen, and we went out and sat on the small front porch and talked, until Jonah yelled my name from inside the house. I rushed in and found him standing in the middle of the kitchen. "You said we'd be runnin' the boat and I'd be the deck man!"

"Yeah, Jonah, I did say that, but y'know, the boat has been stolen, so we have to wait until we get it back."

"When's that gonna be?" he asked.

"I don't know, Jonah, God said we'll get her back, but until then, you'll be my right-hand man, my assistant, and be with me all the time. That sound alright?"

"Sure, Capt. Dor, I'm your right-hand assistant man!"

At about noon, Attorney Bradley called. "Dor, the investigator has found *MacHannah*!"

"Great!" I said. " Where is she?"

"It's back in the boathouse at Woodhill, and Mr. Downey and three of his boat yard employees have been arrested."

"Back at Woodhill? Gee, that's really weird," I said.

"Yes, but it's somewhat clever as well. They must have assumed that nobody would expect it to return there, and sneaked it down the river at night. The investigator said that they were tearing the wheelhouse apart, evidently to re-build it to look different, so no one would recognize it as the old *MacHannah*, I'd guess."

"When can I go get her?"

"The Sheriff's Department Water Patrol has to complete their investigation, so until they're finished with that, it'll be locked-up tight. They will contact me when it's released, and I'll call you right away."

It was turning into a busy day at MacAndrew House. Wil came back from his Pastor's retreat with Katie and three new bairns, Arnold, a tall, thin boy with bright red hair; Kyle, short and muscular; and Danny, nervous and always blinking his eyes. They were all in need of a shower and some clean clothes. I showed them the sleeping area and showers and laid-out their bedding while they washed-up. Katie would have to fit them with what clothes we had left. We'd try washing their clothes later.

"Wil, *MacHannah's* been found!" I gushed.

"That's great, Dor," he said without much enthusiasm.

"What's wrong, man?" I asked.

"You going back on the river?"

"Well, sure," I said. "That's my business - what I do."

"Yeah, well, we sort of thought you'd be runnin' MacAndrew House."

"Well, I can help-out while I'm not runnin' cargo." I felt bad, and I sure wanted someone to run MacAndrew House. Someone who cared as much as the rest of us, but I couldn't just let *MacHannah* sit and rot away, she was a working boat, and needed to be run.

"We'll figure something out," said Wil.

That evening, Wil and Katie, May Sue, her parents, and me, all got together with the eight bairns at Kircaldy Christian Church where Wil and Katie had a dinner and a meeting they called an 'orientation'. I found out that it was a meeting to explain and talk about the rules at MacAndrew House.

The boys got along with each other pretty good. Especially after Katie explained the Merit System, where each bairn would be graded on things like helping, neatness, school grades, cooperation, stuff like that.

"We want to make good citizens out of you, and you'll be rewarded for your good work, just like in the real working world," explained Katie.

"Yeah, sure!" said Chris. "We'll just be slaves, doin' what y'all want us to do all the time, just so we can have a bed!"

I stood up, getting tired of his complaining, but Wil stepped-in first. "Chris, we're no different here at MacAndrew House than anyplace else. All your life, you'll have to work to be able to buy food, and have a place to live, but the difference is, here you'll have help, and you'll learn, and it won't be all work, we'll have fun too. You'll have friends, and people to talk to when you have troubles or worries. That's hard to find in the everyday world out there."

I added, "As far as being 'slaves', you are more like family here." I sat down, my anger gone.

"You'll also learn about the Bible, God, Jesus Christ, and the Holy Spirit. All these things will make you a better person, a better citizen, and hopefully you'll have a place in Heaven reserved just for you." said Katie.

Chris just sat looking down at the floor.

We were all together again the next morning, Sunday, at Kircaldy Christian Church. Wil's sermon on David and Goliath from 1 Samuel 17, held the bairn's interest. Even Chris paid attention.

After the service, Chris came to me, "What's that 'sling' thing he was talking about?"

"Well Chris," I explained, "In early Biblical times, the sling was used to throw rocks far and fast as a weapon. The bow and arrow wasn't even invented yet, so whole armies were armed with stones and slings. It is said they were accurate to even more than 100 yards!"

"Can you make one for me?"

"Well the early slings were made of leather or woven wool with a center pocket for the stone. It shouldn't be too hard to make one."

Back at MacAndrew House, I made a crude

sling from the tongue of an old shoe we found in the trash, and a piece of rope.

I told Chris, "So that they all went the same distance, the rocks should all weigh about the same." So he went to work chipping chunks from the river rocks with a hammer and weighing them on the scale from the kitchen. In the time it took me to make the sling, he had a dozen stones ready for throwing.

Using some of the other rocks, I showed him how to place the stone in the pocket, grip the two ends of the rope and swing it in a circle, and letting go of one end of the rope, sending the rock hurling off across the corral.

Remember Chris," I warned him, "this here thing can kill a person and do some real damage to a house or car, or just about anything , so don't ever toss a rock at anything that will be hurt if you hit it, okay?"

"Okay, Dor,' said Chris. "But we'll sure be safe from giants from now on!"

I wandered back down to the church and found Wil showing Arnold, Kyle and Danny how to straighten-up the church after the service. "Hi, Wil." I said. "When you get a few minutes, I got somethin' I want to talk to you about."

We sat in his little office. "Wil, how about if Walter comes to MacAndrew House when I'm away runnin' on the river, and teaches the bairns how to draw and paint and print like he does?"

"That would be good for the bairns and Walter

too!" he said. "I'll call Attorney Bradley in the morning and see if he can do without your daddy when
he's needed here."

So it was all set, I could go back to running
MacHannah and Walter would fill-in for me at the
House, and I would pay him for his time.

The Sheriff's Department Water Patrol released *MacHannah* to us the next Wednesday, and
Attorney Bradley had it towed back to Duke Farley's
boatyard in Quickville. The wheelhouse had been
taken down to be replaced with a different-looking
one so it wouldn't be recognized. A lot of the trim
and windows and outside woodwork had been re-
moved, and it had started to be re-painted different
colors. Duke and his son, Malcomb, immediately
started re-building the wheelhouse, and Wil promised to spend a couple of hours a day painting -- a
job he did well and enjoyed doing. I stayed busy at
MacAndews House.

At night I prayed, thanking God for MacAndrew
House, my friends, the bairns, and praying that he
would continue to bless us all.

And I looked to my light, but it was not there.

Chapter Twelve

**"Suppose one of you has a
hundred sheep and loses one
of them. Doesn't he leave the
ninety-nine in the open country and go after the lost sheep
until he finds it?"   Luke 15:4**

Summer came to the river early. Flocks of birds
swept across the sky, coming back from their win-
ter homes, and the river got bigger and ran faster,
putting pressure on the levees as the snow up north
melted.

I drove my old Ford that I didn't use very often,
over to Kirkcaldy Christian Church. No one was
there, so I left the keys and a note to Wil telling him
that it could be used for whatever it was needed for
at MacAndrew House. Then I walked over there.

The bairns were getting along with each other pretty well. There hadn't been a real fight, for
weeks, just some yelling. For the most part, they
seemed to be working hard, learning, and starting
to actually enjoy being at MacAndrew House. They
had Bible study every other evening.

I was able to work on *MacHannah* for a few

hours each day, then work at the House until late at night. The bairns didn't help me much, I guess they figured that they worked enough during the day.

Chris still kept to himself. The others called him 'The Loner' and he was fine with that title. I worried that giving him the rock-tossing sling had been a bad thing to do, but he has proved to be responsible with it. I haven't ever had to get on him about it.

Walter showed up and began to get to know the bairns and get familiar with his duties at MacAndrew House. He bunked-down in a small room we had set aside for him, and was eager to help us out.

Every night and every morning, I'd look in on Walter and the bairns to see that they were okay, and to say 'good night' or 'good morning' to them. One very sunny and bright morning I went in to wake-up the bairns and saw Harry's bedding all folded nicely. He wasn't to be found, so I went out to the shed where Chris was still sleeping.

"Hey, Chris," I said. "Have you seen Harry?"

He scrubbed his eyes with his knuckles and squinted up at me, "Yeah. He went out through the corral gate real late last night."

"Which way did he go?"

"I don't know, man, I thought he was just going out for some exercise or somethin'. I went to sleep."

I told my pop, "I'm goin' to go look for Harry. You goin' to be okay here alone?"

"Son, I ain't alone, I got a whole house full of

boys here to keep me company!" He was laughing as I went out the back door.

At the corral I found footprints in the dirt where Harry had struggled with the big, wooden gate, and then he shuffled off toward Quickville to the south. After changing clothes, gathering up some food to take with me, and letting Sheriff Sardino know what I was doing, I hurried off after Harry.

There was a good chance that I'd never find him, but I had to try. Harry had a problem talking to people, so I wondered how he ever got anyone to give him food or anything, and I also worried about why he decided to leave MacAndrew House.

From the moment I went through the corral gate, I began to pray. I prayed that God would direct me to Harry, that he'd be okay, and that I could help him. I figured if he didn't want to come back to MacAndrew House, I couldn't force him to, but I really wanted to know if I could correct whatever it was that made him want to leave.

He had traveled during the night, so I figured that he'd go around the dense and scary clump of trees I came to. I tried to picture it being dark, and which way he would go. I figured that the moon would be lighting the east side of the trees, so I went that way, praying, and watching the ground for his tracks.

Down in a little gully, I found the still warm ashes of a small campfire, and signs that someone had spent some time there. They, or he, couldn't have been gone for very long, so I kept going.

I thought back to about five years before, when I, just like Harry, had run away from Pastor Mac, the man who had saved my life and had taken care of me. I had ended-up aboard Captain Jonathan Hannah's work boat *Killdeer*, and learned the riverboat business. Leaving Pastor Mac worked-out well for me back then, but it's for sure that things don't work-out the same for everybody, and Harry may not be as lucky as I was.

I stayed up on the hill that ran above and behind Quickville, and looked-down at the town. I thought that Harry would not go down into town, some folks there would know him. I kept heading southerly until I came to a well-kept small ranch-style house and barn with a shiny white fence all around it. I remembered that the barn was where I slept the first night after I left Pastor Mac.

As before, there didn't seem to be anyone there. No cars in the driveway, no smoke coming out of the chimney, all the doors were closed, and curtains were pulled across all the windows. I squeezed between the rails of the fence, and headed for the barn.

There were no wheel, horse, or foot tracks in the dirt, except for one trail of small footprints, scuffing along the side of the barn to the door where I had entered some six years before. I very carefully opened the door and peeked around the corner of the first horse stall. The horses saw me and became restless, neighing and clattering their stall reins.

A head popped-up from the next stall and the big, startled eyes of Harry stared at me, and as I suspected, he didn't say a word.

"Hey, Harry, it's me, Dor." He just stared at me, "you okay, pal?" He nodded his head up and down twice.

"Well, we were all worried about you, so I came to see if you're okay." He stepped out of the stall and came over to me. I was casually leaning against the wall, trying to keep things calm and quiet, so he'd know I wasn't there to threaten him.

"Harry," I said. "If you don't talk to people, they can't help you. I like you, man, so why don't you tell me what it is about living at MacAndrew House that you don't like. Nobody else has wanted to leave, and I don't know what I can do to make you happy there."

He sat down on a bale of hay and looked up at me scared-like. "Ith's the way I talk," was all he said.

"Wadda ya mean?" I asked.

"I lispth. Other boys make fun of me, stho I don't talk."

"Well, Harry, we...." I started.

"Iths werry hard for folkths to unnerstan me, Dor." He looked very sad, and I didn't know what to say. Lisping is a problem I'd never run into before, but I really wanted to help this kid.

"Okay, Harry, I understand better now, and I promise you that if you come back to MacAndrew

House with me, I'll find some sort of doctor, or some-one who will help you get rid of that lisping, okay?"

"Ahwight, Dor," he mumbled, "But iths the oth-er boyths that makths fun of me."

"I'll put a stop to that!" I promised. "Let's have a prayer, and then go home, pal."

We stopped at Wil and Katie's house, and they were happy to see Harry back. After I explained his problem, Katie said, "Okay, Dor, Harry will stay with us. We have an empty room upstairs, and that way the other bairns won't pick on him."

Wil agreed with enthusiasm, so Harry had a new home, and I headed for *MacHannah*.

Duke and his son, Malcomb, had the front wheelhouse windows and framing replaced, and had started on the sides of the wheelhouse and cabin. It would look almost as it had before it was taken apart by the thieves to disguise it. One thing that I was happy about, was that when *MacHannah* was found, the River Patrol recovered the beautiful name plaque that Attorney Bradley had made for us. I would put it back up on the front of the cabin as soon as Farley and his son were finished with the repairs.

I fell into the bed, almost too tired to say a prayer, but I did. I thanked God for helping me find Harry, and prayed that he'd be cured of his lisp. I also prayed for all of the bairns, for Wil and Katie, for my pop, Attorney Bradley, and especially for Mary Sue, who I really missed. I fell asleep with her on my mind.

The old river stretched-out ahead, and I was aboard *Killdeer*, and I saw Captain Hannah was at the wheel. "I yelled at ye last time, boy, and you deserved it!"

I wondered if he knew how badly it hurt me to have him mad at me -- but he was mostly mad at everyone, all the time.

"But the Devil take me if'n I'm lyin' to ye...You done good getting ole *MacHannah* workin' back on the river!"

He turned toward me, his eyes blazing like coal fire, "Still and all, you bone-brained barrel of hog slop, you lost my *Killdeer*, you did! Blast your mangy hide!"

He slowly faded away, and I was back in the bunk on *MacHannah*. I laid there, thinking about what he said, and realized that was the first time he'd ever sort-of apologized, and that made me happy, even if it was in a dream. Then, he yelled at me like old times, and that didn't surprise me.

I dozed-off again, and there, like a faint glint of a gold nugget on black velvet, was my Light! It slowly grew, coming closer, changing shape, scaring me some, until I saw it begin to transform into the clad-in-white, shining image of Pastor MacAndrew.

"Aye, me laddie!" He said. "It's proud I am of ye for goin' after the wee bairn, 'arry!"

I said something to him, but I guess he couldn't hear it, because he went on, "Have no fear, me boy. 'arry will nae suffer with the demon of speech much longer. Your faith and prayers will heal. Did ye be knowin' that, lad?"

I started to say that no, I didn't know that, but he had already begun to fade back into the distance, until he was just a small nugget of gold on that vast plain of black velvet.

Morning creeped in, hidden in a shroud of fog. It was dead still. The crickets, and toads, and crows, were as quiet as the moss hanging from the trees. I went to the wheelhouse. With the windows still not put in, everything was damp with morning dew. I heard a soft knock on the hull.

"Dor, it's me, Wil. You up yet?"

"Well, Wil, if I wasn't, I'd sure be now. What's goin' on?"

"Trouble at MacAndrew House," said Wil. "The bairns have been fightin' and they trashed the place!"

"Let's go!" I grabbed up my jacket and Wil started the old Ford and we headed for the home.

"What caused the fightin'?" I asked.

"Dont Know. None of us was there."

"Where was Walter? He's suppose to be there when I'm away."

"Well, if you remember, you left in a hurry to go find Harry, and Walter didn't even know you was gone, so he went into town. Mary Sue was too far away to get here before today, and Kate and me was out of town."

"I told Sheriff Sardino that I had to go," I explained.

"Well, that's fine, but he has work to do too, and was really busy with his Sheriffin' in town."

"Yeah, I guess with you and me and Walter gone, and the Sheriff busy, the bairns didn't go to work yesterday, right?"

"Right." nodded Wil. "And they got bored, I guess, and tore up the place."

Wil pulled-in and parked the old ford, and we went in. One bunk bed was on its side with a leg broken off, and the others were shoved around, out of place. The bedding was in piles, and it looked like they had a water fight as well. Everything was sopping wet. We went out to the corral looking for the bairns. "Jonah! Hey, Davey! Larry! Arnold, Kyle, Danny! Come on out, boys!"

There wasn't anyone around, and I actually missed the sound of Jonah's screeching harmonica. Even Chris' shed was empty, his bedding neatly laid-out on his rolled-up mattress, his 'David's sling' on top of it.

"Looks like they all left," said Wil.

I could feel the anger tightening my gut, and I let it out by blurting, "Well, they can all go to the devil for all I care! They have no appreciation for anyone's caring for them, so I'm done caring!" I immediately felt bad for my lack of patience, and muttered, "Sorry, Wil. I guess I really don't mean that."

He grinned at me, "You only said what I was thinking, pal!"

We went on to Wil's house where there was a message from Attorney Bradley. He had a contract to take a load of goats from Barriston to Lewisport in a week and wanted to know if *MacHannah* would be ready to go. I called Duke Farley at the boatyard, and then Attorney Bradley in Barriston. "She'll be ready," I promised Attorney Bradley. "I'm eager to get back to work on the river!"

I'd go even if *MacHannah* was still in pieces!

Wil and I worked on *MacHannah* until dark, never even mentioning MacAndrew House or the bairns.

I showered, and sat on the bed, reading the Bible. I was in Colossians 3:12-13, where it says; *Therefore, as God's chosen people, holy and dearly loved, clothe yourselves with compassion, kindness, humility, gentleness and patience. **13**Bear with each other and forgive one another if any of you has a grievance against someone. Forgive as the Lord forgave you.*

I again felt badly for being so angry with the bairns, and prayed that I'd be forgiven and given more patience with them.

As I slipped into sleep, I felt the Lord speak to me, not in words, but in what I can only describe as a 'sensation.' I knew, but didn't know *how* I knew, he said; *Through Me and the Holy Spirit that lives in you, all your sins are forgiven.*

Chapter Thirteen

**Go out to the flock and bring
me two choice young goats, so
I can prepare some tasty food
for your father, just the way
he likes it.**
Genesis 27:9

Wil and I worked on *MacHannah* all of that
weekend, getting her ready to make the run up to
Barriston and take the load of goats to Lewisport.
On Monday, Duke Farley and his son almost had the
wheelhouse finished, and it looked great. Wil was
painting it.

"Ahoy the *MacHannah!*" Someone yelled. I
heard Wil laugh, and as I came out of the wheelhouse, I saw Mary Sue and Katie, both dressed like
pirates, and carrying a big picnic basket.

"Looks like the ladies have brought us some
lunch!" said Wil.

We sat and ate, talked and laughed. Everyone
was in good spirits, until I asked about MacAndrew
House, and if the bairns had come back, then it got

real quiet.

"What are we going to do?" asked Katie.

"Well," said Wil. "I think we have to sit down and decide if we're going to continue with MacAndrew House, or give it up."

"I can't give up on those kids, Wil." I said.

Mary Sue and Katie both agreed. "We'll just clean the place up and go find the boys, or other boys. Lord knows, there's lots of kids that need help." said Mary Sue.

"I gotta get me a new deckhand, I guess." I said. Just then someone stumbled out of the brush alongside the boatyard. It was Pete! "Hey, Pete!" I yelled, "C'mon over here, man!"

Pete slowly walked over and sat down on an old upturned paint can. "Wa'cha all doin'?" he asked.

"Gettin' *MacHannah* ready for a run up to Barriston and Lewisport," I told him. "Got a load of goats."

"Goats?" He looked shocked. "You ever carry goats before?"

"Nope, but right now, I'd take on a load of rattlesnakes." Pete just shook his head.

"Lookin' for a job, Pete?" I asked.

"Sure I am, but I'm not sure I want to take on a load of goat."

"Well, I can use you if you want to go with me."

"With *us*!" said Mary Sue.

That surprised me, so she went on, "I'd like to go with you, Dor, if it's okay. I can help out. You'll need some help since Jonah's gone."

"Okay. Sure, Mary Sue." I said it kind of quiet like, but inside I was jumping up and down.

"Pete, you're amazin', man," I said. "You always show up when I need you. How do you do it?"

He shrugged and said, "It's like you said, Captain, I'm amazin'!"

Duke Farley and his son, Malcomb, had the wheelhouse pretty well finished, so we left Quickville the next day after buying rolls of fencing and some wood and nails. We'd need that stuff to keep the goats corralled in the cargo area. We'd arrive in Barriston late that night, load the goats the next morning, and head on upriver to Lewisport. The river was over its spring thaw flooding, and was running easy. We'd make good time upstream, I figured.

"I hope you're not mad at me for inviting myself on this run, Dor," said Mary Sue.

"Gosh, no, Mary Sue, I like havin' your company. It gets pretty lonely up here sometimes."

"I was hoping that we could be together more at MacAndrew House, but that didn't happen." She sat close to me on the helmsman's seat.

"Aw, yeah," I mumbled. "Lookin' for *MacHannah* took up a lot of my time."

Nightime on the river can be beautiful, especially when there's a big, full moon. Its reflection on the water ahead of the boat makes a shimmering, silvery road, and the trees along the banks create strangely-shaped shadows that dance along the water's edge on both sides of the boat. It's pretty quiet. Only the chugging of the engines, and the splashing of the bow wake can be heard, and Mary Sue and me didn't talk much. We just enjoyed the ride.

Pete came up into the wheelhouse. "How many?" He asked.

"How many what?"

"Goats, man," he said. "We're goin' to pick up a load of goats, ain't we?"

"Oh, sure." I thought I'd kid him a little, "There's sixty-three and a half."

"Sixty-three and a *half?*" He rubbed his neck and squinted at me. "How you gonna get *half* a goat?"

"Oh," I said. "That's simple...One of the nanny goats is about ready to have a kid!"

"And if the kid is born before we get the load to Lewisport," said Mary Sue. "We get a bonus for delivering more than we started out with."

"Ah," said Pete, "Y'all were kiddin' me, weren't you."

"Nope," I said. "The nanny goat is doin' the *kiddin'!*"

Pete looked sort of confused for awhile, and then suddenly said, "Now, I got it. What you're sayin' is that the baby goat is a *kid*, and so when the nanny goat has her baby, she'll be doin' the *kiddin'*... not you...that right?"

"No kiddin'," I said. Mary Sue went to laughing,

and Pete left the wheelhouse mumbling to himself.

"How many goats -- *really*?" asked Mary Sue.

"Gosh, I don't know," I said. "No kiddin!"

We docked in Barriston at about midnight had a light dinner in a small cafe that just about to close as we got there. Mary Sue explained to the owner that we had just docked and hadn't eaten all day. He let us in, locked the door behind us and said, "What'll you have?"

We got about five hours of sleep before they came to load the goats. Pete had the cargo deck all fenced-in and had even made a gate at the back with hinges and a latch and everything.

"How many goats ya got?" I asked the fore-man.

"By my count, forty-eight, more or less."

I had Pete and Mary Sue get an accurate count in case they claimed some were missing when we got to Lewisport. Turns out, there were exactly forty-eight.

Pete was looking at each goat very carefully. "What'cha lookin' for, Pete?" I asked.

"Well, I'm lookin' for that pregnant goat, Dor!"

May Sue went into another fit of laughter.

The goats were restless, jumping up and down and butting each other with their heads. And the noise of their stomping around and bleating. Some amazing sounds came out of the cargo area, all of them made by the goats. One sounded like a cluck-ing chicken, another, like a baby crying, and there was a honking noise, grunts and whistles -- through the goat's nose!

Their constant butting of each other, the fence and the gate, gave me some worry, but Pete said he'd handle them and keep them corralled.

We got underway about 10 a.m., again heading upstream for Lewisport. The goat's noise got so annoying that I closed the aft wheelhouse door leading down to the cargo deck. That was better.

Mary Sue was on the foredeck, enjoying the sunshine and reading or writing something. Seems that she is always either reading or writing, but I've never seen what it is that she reads, or writes.

I heard a rumbling noise, Mary Sue screamed, and I heard Pete start yelling at something. Then I saw that he was yelling at Mary Sue and the goats were charging up the side deck, heading for the bow where she was.

Pete was in the middle of the herd of bleating animals, trying hard not to have his feet stomped on with their sharp hoofs, as he headed for May Sue. She jumped up on the rail before Pete got to her. The stampeding herd of goats went on by, clattering down the other side deck. Pete saw a break in the crush of kicking, butting, and snorting beasts, and hurried Mary Sue to the safety of the wheelhouse.

"You okay, Mary Sue?" Then I asked, "Pete, what happened? The corral break-down?"

"Yup, them smelly critters done kicked the slats right outta the gate I made and took-off arunnin' around the decks. I'm sorry Dor, but man, them's harder to handle than I thought they would be!"

"Well, just try to keep them from fallin' overboard, okay, Pete?"

"Sure, Dor, I'm on it!" And he hurried back down to the mass of hairy critters milling around the deck, eating the hay bales and flags, and rope... anything and everything!

"I'm sorry Mary Sue, but I don't know nothin' 'bout goats or any other kind of animal, actually!"

She laughed. "Nobody does, Dor!" She layed her pad and pen on the chart table.

"What are you writin'?"

"Oh, I like to do silly poetry. It's not very good, but it's fun to make rhymes."

"Can I see it?" Without a word, she handed me the paper, and stood aside, smiling. I read;

Here's my advice to you with boats,
Don't go up the river,
With a load of goats.

They kick and they bite,
Their noise is a fright,

They have a strange smell,
So that it is easy to tell,
On your boat they mustn't dwell.

So, to avoid all their muck,
Ship them by truck!

"Ah Ha!" I laughed. "That's really terrific. I don't know nothin' about poetry, but I like that poem!"

"It's sort of a hobby for me," she explained.

"Do you have any more poems?"

"Yes, I have a notebook almost full."

I could hear Pete down on the cargo deck yelling at the goats. He'd go running around the side deck, across the foredeck and down the opposite side deck, waving a red towel, and making all kinds of crazy noises. Finally, he had them all rounded-up and back in the cargo area. He came up to the wheelhouse, all out of breath.

"You're sure earnin' your pay on this trip, Pete," I said.

"Phew," he puffed. "Them's the goofiest animals I ever did see!" He was rubbing his backsides.

"You get hurt?" I asked.

"Yeah, those onery, lop-eared devils keep rammin' their heads into my be-hind!"

Mary Sue and me were trying not to laugh, and were glad when Pete decided to go back down to the cargo deck.

"He'll have bruises, I'd bet," said Mary Sue.

"Yeah, probably, but I don't want to see 'em!"

Just then, the wheelhouse door banged open and a black and white, bearded billy goat came in. Mary Sue jumped up on the chart table, and I just stood there, not knowing what to do. The old goat took a run at me, but I dodged him and he stopped by the side door, just looking at me like I was his next meal.

I quickly checked the river ahead, adjusted our course a bit, and looked back just in time to see the billy goat running at me. I jumped to the door to the lower cargo deck where he had come in, and jerked it open just as he butted me, sending me hurling down the ladder, landing on top of a bunch of other goats. The billy goat came down the ladder like he climbed ladders every day, and I leapt over him and raced back up to the wheelhouse, by bottom aching.

Mary Sue had the helm, and I could see that we had clear water ahead, as I rammed a chair under the doorknob to lock the crazy goat out.

"Thanks for taking the helm, Mary Sue," I said.

She was grinning and said, "How's your bottom, Captain?"

With no comment, I took the helm and busied myself making entries in the log book.

As the night took the river and *MacHannah* into its velvet arms, the goats quieted down, and things got back to normal. Mary Sue was tired, and went below to her bunk. Pete sat on the foredeck, watching the river banks pass by and enjoying the sparkling river as it passed under *MacHannah's* bottom.

I, with my bottom throbbing, stood at the helm, guiding the old workboat on its way upstream toward the docks at Lewisport.

In the quiet, I prayed for Pete, Wil and Kate, Walter, Mrs. MacAndrew, Attorney Bradley, each of the bairns, and prayed for their safe return to their MacAndrew House. The river ahead was clear of any boat traffic, so I closed my eyes and prayed that God would continue to lead and direct us, keeping us safe and providing for us. I also spoke of Mary Sue and my feelings for her, and asked God to show me his Light if he approved.

The blackness of my sight was slowly pierced by a pin-point of light that grew, went off, then back on.

I opened my eyes, knowing that my feelings for Mary Sue were approved by our God in Heaven, and the Holy Spirit within me! The boat was exactly on course, and now I felt that my life was back on course too!

Chapter Fourteen

**Blessed are those who have
learned to acclaim you,
who walk in the light of your
presence, Lord.**
Psalm 89:15

P ete had to replace two of the dock lines the goats chewed-up, but we had *MacHannah* docked and secure without waking Mary Sue. The goat cargo was quiet, and I stretched-out in the wheelhouse to sleep, while Pete wanted to continue laying-out on the foredeck, looking up at the starry night sky.

I woke up in the morning to find that the goats had been unloaded by Pete and the shipping company, and the paperwork was in his hands, all signed, sealed and delivered. "How's your backside feelin' today, pal?" I asked him.

"Like I been hit by a train!" he replied. "How's yours?"

"Same train," I replied with a moan. We sat on the pier, waiting for Mary Sue. We would go to breakfast, then begin the trip back downriver to Quickville.

After breakfast, we got *MacHannah* ready and pulled out of Lewisport and into the rapidly-moving flow. The river narrowed just above Lewisport and the current sped-up for about four miles, until the river widened again to the south. I never understood why a river port would be placed at that fast-running spot. Mary Sue said that there was once a mill there, and it needed the fast-moving current. I am always amazed at how smart she is.

"Here's my notebook, Dor," she said. "If you want to look at any of my silly poems, it's alright, just don't make fun of me, okay?"

I agreed, and opened the notebook to the middle. I put it down so that I could read it and still run *MacHannah*, and watch ahead. I read a couple of poems. One I didn't understand. Then, I came to one I did understand;

DORKY

He's Dorky, but I love him just the same.
He's Dorky -- it's his God-given name.

Honest, brave and true,
He'll give his all for you.

And to me he'll always be,
Tall and sturdy as a tree.

So I certainly declare,
That I'd go anywhere,

With Dorky...
My handsome Teddy bear.

I didn't mind being her 'Teddy bear,' In fact I kind of liked it.

The run downstream to Quickville was the fastest I'd ever made. We didn't even have to stop for fuel. As we pulled up to the pier in the slough next to the boat yard, it was well before the evening wrapped the river in its blanket of black.

Wil and Katie picked-up Mary Sue. They said that a speach therapist was seeing Harry, and he was making progress. I told Mary Sue that I liked the Dorky poem, but hadn't read all the rest of them yet. She told me to keep the notebook for her. That would give her a reason to come back. She hurried to go, but not before she gave me a good-night kiss!

Pete had everything tied down and secure, so I paid him and thanked him, and he said, "I'll amaze you again, soon as you have another run planned!" I knew he would.

I was tired, but felt good as I showered and crawled into the bunk. It had been a good run, pretty much trouble-free, and I'd learned a bit about goats as cargo.

"Thank you Father," I prayed aloud. "Thank you for being with us on this run, and thank you for Mary Sue and Pete." I had my eyes closed, and felt -- I can't explain how -- that God was there in the boat's small cabin with me.

"I'm worried about the bairns, Father, they need to be someplace safe and healthy like McAndrews House, and I feel like I let them down by being away, and I pray that you'll watch over them, as you have watched over us."

In the distance, I could see the small speck of light that is my Light. "God," I continued, "Please bring the boys back to us, or, if it's what you want, send us some new boys, bairns, that we can help through their tough times." My Light was steady, still far off, and I wondered if I was still being heard.

"Dear Lord, I'm thinking that MacAndrew House was something that you wanted us to do, is that right?" My Light blinked off, then on again. "And I guess the reason the bairns tore up the place and left, was that they were unhappy because of something we did. Is that right?" The light stayed steady.

"No? What was it then; the food, the beds, the clothes, were we too strict, not strict enough?" My Light never changed.

"Oh, I sure wish I could ask them," I muttered, and the light suddenly blinked off and on. "Well, I guess what you're telling me is that I have to find them and ask them, right?" My light blinked again, and then slowly faded into the darkness. I knew what I needed to do. I must find the bairns and talk to them. That's the way, the only way, I can correct the MacAndrew House problem. I prayed until I fell asleep.

In the morning, I mailed the goat run paperwork to Attorney Bradley, and went to see Wil at Kirkcaldy Church. He didn't have any idea where to start looking for the bairns, but I did. I got the keys to the old

Ford from him, filled-up the gas tank, and headed for Nussome, a medium-size town east of Quickville. If I was all alone again, it's where I would go to find some work, or another home for boy's. There were two of them there.

I pulled into Nussome and parked the Ford at one end of the main street that was only about eight blocks long, and began to walk slowly into the downtown area, checking the alleys as I went. About four blocks into town, I saw the rear end of a boy hanging over the side of a trash bin, searching through the garbage and trash, probably looking for food. It looked like it might be Arnold, one of the boys Wil found and put to work at the church.

"That you in there, Arnold?" The boy jerked like someone smacked him with a wet fish, turned, and jumped -- almost fell -- from the edge of the dumpster. Before he could run-off, I grabbed his shirt tail.

"Whoa, pal," I said calmly, "it's just me, Dorky Walker, from the MacAndrew House!"

"Oh. Hi, Captain Walker." He leaned back against the trash container, looking at me like a rabbit looks at a fox. "You gonna take me back there?"

"That's up to you, man. I ain't gonna do nothin' you don't want me to do. I just want to talk with you for a minute." He nodded his head and relaxed a bit.

"I didn't tear-up the House, sir."

"Well, don't worry about that. Nothin' was done that can't be undone. I just want to know why the bairns done that."

"I don't know." He was looking down at the dirt, and I saw that his clothes were as dirty as they were when he first came to MacAndrew House.

"Well," I continued, "we'd sure like to know what was botherin' y'all. And we'd like you to come back. It sure beats digging in garbage for your food, don't it?"

He nodded his head, and I wondered what it was that made this boy so sad. "Arnold, us folks at MacAndrew House just want to give you guys a good home. Someplace where you'll be happy and well taken care of. We'd like to see you to grow up to be good, God-fearin' citizens. Understand?"

Again he just nodded his head.

"Do you know where the other bairns are?"

He hesitated long enough that it told me that he surely did know where they were. "Well, look, I'll be goin' back to MacAndrew House now, but if you see any of the other boys, would you tell them what I said, and that we want them to come back to some hot meals, warm comfortable beds, and people who care about them. We're not mad about the mess y'all left, so, can you please ask them, for me, to come home?"

Again, Arnold just nodded, but I could see a tear running down his cheek, so I gave him a hug. He held on tightly for a long time. I walked back to the Ford, sat and prayed for the bairns and for all the lost, forgotten kids wandering around with no one to take care of them, and no one to love them. Then I turned it around and headed back to Quickville.

At MacAndrew House, I came up behind Walter as he was busy cleaning-up the place, making beds, and repairing broken chairs and bed frames. "Hi, pop!" He jumped like someone poked him.

"Whoa! Howdy, son," he almost yelled. "Where ya been?"

"Just been goin' 'round sneakin' up on folks and scarin' them." I told him. "Took a load of goats up to Lewisport, and I been over to Nussome lookin' for the bairns."

"Find 'em?"

"Found one; little ol' Arnold. He promised to try to get the others to come back. How you doin', pop?"

"Fine, just fine, son." He stopped what he was doing and smiled, saying, "I ain't never been more happy than I am now, workin' here with you, Wil and Katie, and especially ol' Bradley. Y'all got me off the booze, and I'm right thankful for that."

"Well, we're right thankful to have you here too, pop." I helped him fold up some bedding and pick up the trash that was under the bedding, "I'll see you tomorrow. G'night."

For the next three days, I didn't have time to think about anything except getting *MacHannah's* cabin and painting finished, and cleaning up the smelly mess left by the goats. Wil came and worked awhile almost every day, and he told me that Mary Sue had been busy every day at MacAndrew House, doing cleaning and fixing meals for pop and whoever else was there at eating time. I decided that I'd like to go see her. So I did.

Wil was using the old Ford, so I walked over to MacAndrew House the next morning. Mary Sue insisted that I have some breakfast; bacon and eggs, and a blue berry muffin, and it was good.   While I was sitting back, relaxing with a cup of coffee, she suddenly screamed. I jumped to my feet and ran to her in the other room. "What's the matter?"

She was backed-up against the pantry door, pointing toward the back door. I ran to the door, and there was Arnold, Larry, Danny, Kyle, with Davey and Jonah bending over someone, or something.

"Chris is really sick, Dor!" Said Davey.

I hurried down the porch steps to take a look at Chris. He was on his knees, pale, and had been throwing-up. It was all over the front of his shirt and pants. I went back in the house, called Sheriff Sardino, because Chris and Davey were his bairns working at the Sheriff's Station.

"I'll be right there, Dor!" He promised.

I told Mary Sue, "What you saw was the Bairns bringing Chris back here. He's really sick, and Sheriff Sardino is coming to get him, probably to take him to the hospital."

"I'm sorry, Dor. I just saw a dirty face looking through the window!"

I hugged her, "That sure would scare a person, but it's okay now."

The Sheriff was there in only a few minutes, and lifted Chris into the back seat of the police car.

"I'll run him over to Duvalle, that's the closest hospital," he said, and sped off.

Mary Sue swung the kitchen door open and said, "Y'all come on in here and have some breakfast. My goodness, you look like you haven't ate in a week."

I heard Jonah's squeaky harmonica playing an unrecognizable tune.

The boys ambled up into the kitchen.

"Go on now and wash-up, it'll be ready in a few minutes," said Mary Sue.

I walked with them into the bunk area. "Wow!" said Davey. "It's all cleaned up. Looks just like it did before."

"Yeah," I said. "It wasn't all that bad. We had it all back in shape in no time." I noticed that each boy went to his own bunkbed. "You might as well stay here where you all have food, showers, jobs, and people who love you. Wadda ya think?"

They looked at each other, and I felt that they silently agreed that this would be best for them. "Get to washin' up, lads, then come eat."

At the table, I prayed, "Dear Father in Heaven, thank you for bringing the bairns back to MacAndrew House, and for watching over them while they were gone. We pray that Chris will recover well and thank you for all the blessings you so generously provide for all of us. We send this prayer in Jesus' Holy name, Amen."

Jonah stayed and helped Mary Sue clean-up the place, and the others each went to their jobs; Kircaldy Church, the Sheriff's office, and Mason Quick's *Quickville Courier* newspaper.

"Can I still be the 'deck man' on your boat, Dor?" asked Jonah.

"Sure, Jonah," I told him, "Unless you decide to run-off again. Y'know, I need a deck hand that I can depend on being there when we have a cargo."

He nodded and said, "I'll be there, Captain Dor, I promise."

Mary Sue and I sat out on the porch, having coffee and listening to Jonah slaughter another song on his harmonica. We looked at each other and laughed.

I felt like I had a real family now. The bairns, Mary Sue, pop, Wil and Katie, were the family that I had never had before now. And God is the father of us all, and I even had a brother in Jesus!

Mary Sue must have some how known my thoughts, as she said, "Dor, have you ever thought about being a father?"

I didn't know quite what to say and stuttered, "Ah, w-w-w-well, Y'know, I guess I, ummm, have, a little, but I've been too busy, y'know...to, well, think much about that...y'know, sort of stuff."

"Well," she said, "I think you'd be a wonderful father."

Somewhere in the house, Jonah's harmonica croaked a jumbled tune that matched my nervous and unsure feelings.

Chapter Fifteen

**Bear with each other and
forgive one another
if any of you has a grievance
against someone. Forgive
as the Lord forgave you.**
Colossians 3:13

I was at Chris' bedside. He was sleeping comfortably as the nurse came to check on him. "What's the matter with him, ma'am?" I asked her.

"The doctor will be in to see him in a few minutes, you'll have to ask him." And she hurried out.

That worried me. If she didn't want to talk about it, it must be really serious!

The doctor came in about a half hour later. He knocked on the door lightly, peeked around it, then came on in when he saw me sitting there, looking worried. "Hello, I'm doctor Alexander, who are you?"

"I'm Dorky Walker from MacAndrew House where Chris lives."

"What's 'MacAndrew House?'" He asked. I told him all about it, its history and how it came to be, and how the town of Quickville is helping it along.

"Well, that's good, I guess you'd be his legal guardian, right?"

"Well, doctor, I don't know how 'legal' I am, but we're taking care of eight homeless, orphaned lads at MacAndrew House. This is the first time any of them has been sick."

"I see," he said, and went to check Chris' pulse and blood pressure, and went to pushing on his belly. "You know, that I can't treat a minor without permission from a parent or a legal guardian, you know that don't you?"

"Yessir, I guess I do know that, now."

"Where is this 'MacAndrew House?"

I told him where it is, and about the Kircaldy Church, Sheriff Sardino and the *Quickville Courier's* support of MacAndrew House.

"You have a nurse or anyone trained in medicine there?"

"No, we don't. We haven't had a need until now," I explained.

"Well, Dorky... by the way," he hesitated, smiling, where'd you get that name?"

I gave him a quick run-down on my name, my early life, Pastor Mac and Captain Hannah, and the *Killdeer* and the *MacHannah*, and the history of MacAndrew House. He listened quietly, then said, "I treated some of the passengers from the riverboat *Governor Harlan G.* that you saved. I'll tell you what, I'll come to MacAndrew House once a week and check up on your boys there, will that be okay?"

"Man!" I was excited. "That would be wonder-ful, doctor! Thank you a lot!" Chris moaned, and raised-up on one elbow. "What about him, doctor?"

"Oh, he's okay. You can take him home. Just give him lots of liquids. It was a *staphylococcus bac-terium* that gave him a tummy ache, vomiting, and diarrhea. Don't fed him any spicy food for a couple of days, keep it bland, bread and milk, perhaps."

I didn't tell the doctor that Chris had been eat-ing out of garbage cans while away from MacAndrew House.

Back at MacAndrew House, Chris took a quick show-er and went straight to bed. I prayed for him and all of the bairns, then went to the kitchen to see what there was to eat.

"Hampton Bradley left a message for you at our house," said Katie. She and Mary Sue fixed me a plate of food and a big ice-cold glass of milk. My pop, Walter, was there, looking quite at home.

"Hi, pop," I said.

"Dorky, how y'doin', son?"

"I get this fine food into me and I'll be doin' just fine!"

After eating, Mary Sue, Katie, and me went to Wil and Katie's house, leaving pop to watch over Ma-cAndrew House.

"All the bairns are back, Harry's doing really well with the speech therapist, and Attorney Bradley wants you to call him as soon as you get here," announced Wil. I went straight to the phone.

"Hello, Attorney Bradley, this is Dorky."

"Hello Dorky," he said. "You know, since we've been business associates for more than three years now, you could call me Hampton, y'know."

"Oh, yessir, Attorney Bradley...I mean, Hampton, I'm sorry."

He laughed, "There's nothing to be sorry for. Now listen, Thaddeus Downey is going to trial in Little Rock, Arkansas, on the fifteenth, and we have to be there. I think we should drive up there on the twelfth. That'll give us time to prepare our case."

"That'll be fine, Hampton." I felt funny calling him 'Hampton.'

Mr. Downey was the owner of the boat yard that had *MacHannah* before we bought her. He had stolen it later, and been caught, but not before locking me up in a generator room.

The drive to Little Rock was long, but Hampton Bradley was an interesting man, and we talked of many things. That made the time go faster. He checked us into a hotel, and after eating, we went to bed. The next morning, Attorney Bradley was busy filing all sorts of legal paperwork, so I went to the jail and asked if I could see Mr. Downey. I had really liked him when we met at his boatyard, and he hadn't treated me badly, even though he locked me up when I found he had my boat.

I had to identify myself, and explain why I wanted to see the prisoner. A guard searched me and led me down a long row of iron bars with poor lighting, and men making all sort of comments. I was locked in the cell with him, and Mr. Downey had me sit on the bunk. He was surprised to see me, and immediately began to apologize and explain that he really wasn't very enthusiastic about taking *MacHannah*, but the two men with him made him do it. He owed them money.

"What happened to them?" I asked.

"I didn't know it, honest Dor, but they were wanted on a Federal warrant and were taken to Illinois."

"Well, they sure scared me!"

"I know, and I'm really sorry Dorky, but I also knew that you'd be able to work your way out of that old generator room." He looked really sad.

"If you are turned loose, can you go back to the boatyard and work it?" I asked.

"Yes, the Yard Foreman is taking care of the work right now, but I don't know how long he'll be able handle it."

I went back to Attorney Bradley. "Do you think you can get Mr. Downey out of trouble?"

He looked at me like I just asked him to kiss a frog. "Downey looks as guilty as guilty can be, Dorky," he said with some sadness in his voice.

"I know, but he's really sorry, and I think he was forced into doin' that by the other guys."

He said, "Well, did you know that he was using that old boathouse in Woodhill without the owner's permission?" He sat back and took off his glasses. "That's even another charge to add to the grand theft, kidnapping, burglary, assault, and who knows what all else. What's on your mind, Dorky?"

"Well, he owed those men a bunch of money, and I think he was forced to do all that stuff."

Bradley put his glasses back on, and mumbled, "Well, that'll be up to the judge to figure out if he's guilty or not."

"I just don't feel very good 'bout gettin' him put in jail." I said.

Attorney Bradley looked at me for a long time, then quietly said, "Y'know, Dorky, there are laws to protect people from things that some other people do, or would like to do, to them. Without laws and pun-ishment for those who knowingly break those laws, we'd be like the wild animals in the jungle, preying on each other."

"Sure, but isn't there times when someone breaks the law 'cause they are forced to?" I asked.

"Yes," he said. "And that's a reason for having hearings, and trials, and courts, and judges, and ju-ries -- to find out if there are any mitigating factors that would make someone less guilty."

"Midergrating frackters?"

"That means there may be a certain condition or situation that makes a bad action or mistake seem less serious, sometimes even making it seem excus-able."

"That's what I think!" I almost shouted. "Mr.

Downey was bein' forced by them others to do what they said because he owed them a lot of money for something, and that was the *'midderating fractory.'*.. um... whatever you said... y'know, *excusable!*"

"That's very possible, Dorky," he replied. "But that would be up to the *State* to argue. I'm representing *you*, the victim, that means you were the injured party."

"I wasn't hurt."

"I know. That simply means you were the one who suffered damage, either physically, mentally, emotionally, or financially, by the illegal actions of the defendant, namely, Thaddeus Downey, and you will testify to that."

"What if I just don't go?"

"That would be a violation of the subpoena, and *you'd* be breaking the law."

"What can I do? I'd feel lousy, putting that old man in jail.

"Well, You could tell the judge that Mr. Downey and you have reached an agreement for him to make restitution by repairing the damage to your boat, returning it to its condition prior to the time it was taken, and you don't want to see him punished. But remember, there may be other criminal charges against him."

He pulled at his chin, took off his glasses and rubbed his eyes. "You really want to do this Dorky?" He asked.

"Yeah, I really do."

The next day we spent a lot of time in a little room with the judge, Mr. Downey's lawyer, and attorney Bradley, who sometimes got mad and yelled at the other attorney. They all used words that I'd never heard before, so I really didn't know what was going on. Attorney Bradley stood up, stuffed all of his papers into his briefcase, and said, "Let's go Dorky, we've done all we can do here."

He didn't even say goodbye to the other folks.

He didn't talk much on the way back to Quickville, except for him to tell me to call him 'Hampton' instead of 'Attorney Bradley' every chance he got.

"He's going to jail," said Hampton Bradley. "Not much chance of him doing the repairs to your boat now, I'm afraid."

"Yeah, I figured on that, but I wanted to give him a chance, but it didn't work, did it."

Attorney Bradley -- *Hampton* -- was very quiet the rest of the way. I kept thinking about Mary Sue, *MacHannah*, the Andrews House, and what I should do about all of them. Finally, I asked Attor...*Hampton*, "Wadda think about Mary Sue?"

"Well, Dorky," he said. "She's a very fine young lady." He smiled at me. "If I were you, I'd hang onto her!"

"I was thinkin' the same thing. Do you think I'm too young to get married-up with her?"

His answer was a simple "No." So, I guess I'm not too young to get married-up with her then...If she's willin'.

We rolled into Quickville and Hampton dropped me off at the Gilley house. Once inside, I asked Katie and Wil the same question...about getting married-up with Mary Sue.

"Sure, Dor," said Wil. "She's been awaitin' for you to ask her!"

I never seen no one 'have a fit,' but what Katie went into must have been pretty much what it's like. She began talking so fast I couldn't understand her, and she kept sort-of screaming, like someone was pinching her. I guess she was really excited about my little question.

"Dor!" she finally said. "That's wonderful! We've been praying that you'd ask her. And I do believe that she'll accept!" She did that scream thing again.

I was nervous. I guess I wasn't really totally sure that I should do it, so I said, "Okay, but please don't say anything to Mary Sue about this, okay? I sort of want to surprise her, okay?"

"Okay!" they said together.

Attorney Bradley (I'm sorry, I just can't get into the habit of calling him 'Hampton,' it somehow seems disrespectful) anyway, he called me that night to tell me that he'd received another call for a trip to a resort town to the south called Sebastian Park, to carry a load of caged birds up to Lewisport. The bird's owners are moving them there to a new bird park, and the river route is quieter and safer than trucking them. We had two days to get ready for the trip, just time enough for me to arrange to get a ring, and see if Mary Sue will go on this trip with me.

That night aboard *MacHannah*, the river was quiet except for the croaking of swamp toads and the cackling of tree crows. I prayed long and hard about what I was going to do, and finished with an 'Amen' and then looked to my Light.

It was glittering like that diamond in Mary Sue's new ring, and the blackness of my closed eyes seemed to be more like the night sky; a little bit of blue. "I need to know if what I'm doin' is your will, or am I messin'-up? Holy Spirit, should I ask Mary Sue to get married-up with me?"

My breath went out like a popped balloon when my Light blinked off and on, not once, but twice! Then, out of the darkness came the glittering shapes that grew into images of Pastor Mac, and standing alongside of him, Captain Hannah.

Pastor Mac said, "You'll nae find a more finer Bride, me lad. She's blessed, and a Christian lassie, and will bring you much joy! God bless you, Dorky me boy!"

Captain Hannah didn't have his cane anymore, and he looked less mad than I'd ever seen him. "Well, you've not quite made the mess of everythin' I thought you would, boy, and I wish you well. Take care of your riverboat first, then tend to your life, got it?"

The next thing I knew, it was morning, and the dawn was lighting-up the forward compartment where I slept. It was quiet, and I lay there for awhile thinking of my Light visions, and what Pastor Mac and Captain Hannah had said. I had new confidence now, and hope for the future.

"The run down to Sebastian Park will only take a day," I told Mary Sue. "But it'll be a two-day run all the way upstream to Lewisport, and a day coming back downstream. Can you go?"

And I went to MacAndrews House where Jonah was busy helping Walter, my pop, paint the corral fence. "Goin' on a trip to deliver some birds up to Lewisport, and I need my deckhand. You ready to go Jonah?"

I got two very excited 'yes!' answers. So I went to work making *MacHannah* ready.

We had dinner at the Gilley's that evening, and Katie was as nervous and excited as a loon on a gator's back, and I was really nervous that she'd let-on to Mary Sue that I was going to ask her to marry up with me.

We said 'good night' and Jonah and me went to *MacHannah*, and Wil would bring Mary Sue to the boat in the morning in time for us to head-out for Sebastian Park to pick-up the birds.

In the morning, *MacHannah* was ready to go, engines warmed-up, charts in place, radio frequencies selected, and on-board fuel and water checked. Jonah was squaring-away the deck and suddenly hollered, "Here comes Miss Mary Sue!"

She came aboard looking really pretty, and carrying a big picnic basket that looked pretty pretty too. We said a prayer, and pulled out of the slough, leaving Wil and Katie waving their good byes from the dock. Katie seemed to be crying. I don't know why.

The run down to Sebastian Park was an easy one. The river was running gently, and carried *MacHannah* along like sledding downhill. The loading crew arrived just as we did, and the crates and cages of exotic birds were put aboard quickly and smoothly. We left Sebastian Park's dock that afternoon and began the upstream run for Lewisport.

Mary Sue was busy in the small galley behind the wheelhouse as Jonah came up. "Y'know, Captain Dorky," he said, "Mister Pete didn't show up this time!"

"Yup, Jonah, he didn't, but don't be surprised if we find him somewhere along the way. He's been known to show up at a lot of different places."

Inside of me, I wouldn't mind if Pete didn't come along on this trip. I wanted peace and quiet, especially when I ask Mary Sue about getting married-up with me.

We ran most all night, and Mary Sue stayed close, watching ahead for snags, and making sure, I guess, that I stayed awake. We pulled into a small cove upstream from Barriston, anchored, and had a midnight dinner on the back deck in the moonlight. The soft twitters and songs of the birds on the cargo deck, the cricket's choir, and the frog's strumming, added to the beauty of the night. Jonah ate, then laid his head back and fell asleep in the deck chair at the table. Mary Sue smiled and said, "We got ourselves a tired boy there, Captain!" That was the first time I thought of Jonah as a son.

I couldn't imagine a better time, so as Mary Sue got up to take the plates to the galley, I pulled the little ring box from my pocket, put it on the table and said, "Ummm, Mary Sue, I'd like to know if you'd like to marry-up with me!"

"Oh, Dorky, of course I'll 'marry-up' with you! I've been waiting for you to ask!" She gave me a big hug and kiss and I slipped the engagement ring on her finger. "It's perfect!" she said, all teary-eyed.

We sat and talked until sun-up, and agreed that we'd try to adopt Jonah. Mary sue said, "Doesn't this remind you of the Bible account of Mary and Joseph and the birth of Jesus?

"No. How do you mean?" I asked, confused.

Well, Jesus had a virgin birth, and here we are, going to have a son, Jonah, too!"

"Well, I don't think Jonah is a new Messiah."

Mary Sue smiled, "You never know, Dorky. You just never know!"

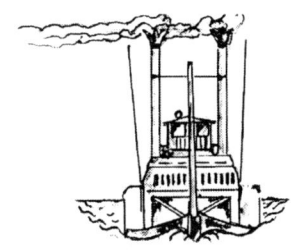

CPSIA information can be obtained at www.ICGtesting.com
Printed in the USA
BVOW05*0502010415

394166BV00003B/8/P